Lady Godiva and other stories

Also by Alberto Moravia

FICTION

The Woman of Rome
The Conformist
Two Adolescents (*Agostino* and *Disobedience*)
The Fancy Dress Party
The Time of Indifference
Conjugal Love
Roman Tales
A Ghost at Noon
Bitter Honeymoon
Two Women
The Wayward Wife
The Empty Canvas
More Roman Tales
The Fetish
The Lie
Command and I Will Obey You
Paradise
The Two of Us

GENERAL

Man as an End
The Red Book and the Great Wall
Which Tribe Do You Belong To?

PLAY

Beatrice Cenci

LADY GODIVA
and other stories

Alberto Moravia

Translated from the Italian by
Angus Davidson

SECKER & WARBURG
LONDON

Published in Italian under the title of *Un' altra vita*
Copyright © 1973 by Casa ed. V. Bompiani

First published in England 1975 by
Martin Secker & Warburg Limited
14 Carlisle Street, London W1V 6NN

English translation copyright
© Martin Secker & Warburg Limited 1975

SBN: 436 28719 6

Printed Offset Litho and bound in Great Britain by
Cox & Wyman Limited
London, Fakenham and Reading

Contents

A SLEEPWALKER

My husband does nothing; I, on the other hand, work: I am a lawyer. But to say that my husband does nothing is incorrect. My husband, it is true, does not work; but he does a great deal, he is one of the busiest men I know. Busy doing what? What indeed! Initiating, planning, developing his numerous love affairs. Being unfaithful to me, in short. Has anyone ever imagined that making love—and with several women at the same time: a short time ago I counted up to eight of them—has anyone ever imagined that this means doing nothing? Anyone who says such a thing does not know what love-making is. Even if it were merely a matter of thinking out stratagems in order to conceal from me and from each of his women in turn that he is being unfaithful, my husband needs the whole of his time, whether free time or not, even if he has actually to rob himself of sleep.

I put up with his deceptions for the first five years of our marriage; then, finally, I decided to have my revenge. I might, of course, have demanded a formal separation; but there was this little drawback—I loved him, and the more unfaithful he was to me the more did my love increase. And so, seeing that the way of separation was barred to me by love, I set out, with the strangely rational logic of passion, upon the path of vengeance. To put it briefly: I decided to kill my husband.

I have one peculiarity: I am a sleepwalker. Often, in the night, I rise from my bed and, with deathly pale face bent forward, dull grey eyes staring, my crisp, electric mop of hair loose over my shoulders, my two hands raised to hold my dressing-gown wide open as though to proffer my neglected body, I prowl about the house. Both my husband and Lena the maid know of my trouble and take good care not to awaken me. Usually I roam through the various rooms, opening drawers, displacing objects, always avoiding, miraculously, any collision with the furniture. Then I go back to bed. My sleepwalking habits are known also to others in the house: one night I walked out on to the landing and went and rang the bell of the apartment next door.

As everyone knows, a sleepwalker may perform highly complicated operations during sleep which, in a state of wakefulness, would demand an awareness and a skill above the normal. In effect, the sleepwalker is like an actor performing a part on the stage, identifying himself with the character he represents in every possible way. In him certain faculties are exalted to the highest extent; others are, as it were, suppressed. And the dream he is experiencing—or, in the case of the actor, the pretence—sharpens his senses, renders his movements precise and infallible. So now I thought I would pretend to have a fit of sleepwalking during which, instead of doing the usual things such as moving chairs, opening doors, fumbling in drawers, I would simply kill my husband by shooting him with a pistol. Sleepwalkers do all sorts of things; after all, it is easier to fire a pistol than to walk along a cornice with outstretched arms. Afterwards, as if nothing had happened, I would go back to bed in my own room. Merely to wake up next morning and find myself, to my own easily credible despair, a widow.

No sooner said than done, and the day was chosen; when evening came I dined alone; my husband, with an improbable excuse (a men-only dinner, all of them graduates of his own faculty in his particular year), had gone out, with one of his women. After dinner I sat in the sitting-room and spent four hours smoking, watching television and skimming through newspapers and magazines. I felt stiff all over, shrunken and benumbed; my head was empty, with no thought in it: perhaps I was already in a state of somnambulism. My husband came in at one o'clock; and, adding injury to insult, did not even look into the sitting-room to give me a goodnight kiss. Instead, he went straight off and shut himself up in his bedroom. I myself, in turn, fled to my own room, undressed, lay down on the bed and spent another four hours smoking in the dark. Strange how there is no enjoyment in smoking unless one can see the smoke. At five o'clock, as I had decided beforehand, I got up from the bed.

I took off my nightdress and slipped on my dressing-gown over my bare body: that is the ritual, it seems, which I observe regularly during my fits of sleepwalking. But on this occasion there was one novelty; my husband's gun, removed that day from the cabinet in which he keeps it, weighed heavy at the bottom of my pocket. I hesitated, then, urged on by will-power, like an actor making his entrance on to the stage, I went to the door, opened it and advanced into the corridor. It is not so much a corridor, to tell the truth, as a kind of narrow passage between two rows of cupboards and shelves full of books. In the feeble light of one or two lamps I then moved forward, stiff as marble, strutting proudly, eyes staring and hair flying loose, holding my dressing-gown open with both hands, my bosom thrust out, my head held back. This was my characteristic manner when sleepwalking, as I knew because both my husband and Lena had many times described it to me.

Step by step I reached the far end of the corridor where was the bedroom of our maid Lena, a tall, lanky, elderly Slav. I thought I would allow her a sight of me so that I would then have some evidence in my favour. Slowly I turned the handle of the door, opened it, looked in, standing stiff and death-like on the threshold. A surprise awaited me. In the indirect light from the corridor Lena's bed was visible, rumpled but empty. The covers were thrown back to one side, as though Lena had got up suddenly. For some reason, I was all at once struck by the disconcerting doubt that some part of my plan was going wrong.

Still walking stiffly, slowly, hieratically like an automaton, I reconnoitred Lena's bathroom and our own: nothing. Where could my servant have gone, at five o'clock in the morning? My suspicion that reality was flawed by some mysterious discrepancy persisted. I decided, nevertheless, to carry on with the execution of my plan even without Lena's evidence. So once again I proceeded along the corridor. As I went I did as I usually do—so they tell me: I stopped, pulled down at random a book from a shelf, opened it, pretended

to read, then put it back in its place. All this in case 'someone' (but who?) might be watching me.

I came to my husband's door. Cautiously I turned the
handle, opened the door and looked in. To my horror there
was Lena, Lena whom I had failed to find, the elderly but
energetic and sprightly Lena—there she was, lying on my
husband's bed. Her bare, bony back and head bristling with
ruffled yellow hair were turned towards the door; and, leaning on one elbow, she was gazing, doubtless with well-justi-
fied satisfaction, at my husband, who was lying flat on his
back, his head on the pillow, his torso uncovered. Once again
I felt that something was going wrong with my plan: I had
not foreseen what I now beheld and, frankly, it was not
foreseeable. But I did not have time to examine this uncom-
fortable feeling carefully. This new, incredible unfaithful-
ness on my husband's part with our servant, with an elderly
woman, with a person, one might say, who was part of the
family, someone whom I trusted and imagined to have
some affection towards me; this improbable betrayal, real
and monstrous as it was and yet logical, had to be punished.
I took hold of the pistol at the bottom of my pocket, slowly
pulled it out and aimed it towards the bed . . . and then I
awoke.

I was standing up, facing the window, leaning with my
elbows on the window-sill, and looking out into the garden.
In front of me was the mass of thick, black ivy that cloaked
the encircling wall. A corner of the garden was visible in
the light from a street-lamp: a marble seat blackened with
damp, the little clump of bay trees surrounding it, the basin
with the jet of water issuing from an artificial rock, rising
slender and bright and then falling back into the dark water.
It was the quietest, the most profound, the most exhausted
moment of the night. If it had not been for the hissing of
the little fountain I might have thought I was dreaming.
Then the cold made me shudder. I pulled the dressing-gown
close over my chest. And then, all of a sudden, I realized
that I had no pistol in my pocket.

It was clear that I had had an attack of sleepwalking. In
my sleep I had risen from my bed, had gone over to the

window, opened the shutters and looked out. But how about my plan to kill my husband by actually pretending to be sleepwalking? It was nothing but a dream within a dream. I had dreamt I was pretending to be dreaming and to be walking about the house as in a dream. But something, during my dream, had made me realize that I was not pretending to be dreaming; but I really *was* dreaming. Of what? Of the incredible, fantastic love affair between my husband and Lena, the crazy conceit of my own paroxysmal, obsessive jealousy.

Nevertheless nothing is certain. It occurred to me that my husband had in truth carried his libertinism to the point of gerontophily, to the forming of a relationship with an elderly domestic servant. Perhaps I really had fired the pistol; perhaps, after firing it, I had dropped it and returned to my room and had there finally woken up. Who could tell? The combination of jealousy and somnambulism, productive of illusions, did not allow me to reject this last possibility. I was now afraid to move away from the window and to go and see 'what' had really happened. So I stayed still, my elbows on the window-sill, looking into the garden. Possibly I was dreaming and had not yet woken up.

A FAMOUS WOMAN

Everything was in order. At the airport, I stopped a short distance from the aeroplane and the group came towards me. There was the blinding light of Africa and I could not see very well. In that light the Africans looked like the dark figures in a photographic negative; as for the Europeans, they positively disappeared, were blurred into the splendour of the sunshine. Nevertheless I recognized the Minister, who greeted me in the name of the Republic which, shortly before, I had visited during a tourist trip; and there were three or four photographers standing or kneeling and frantically taking photographs; two or three journalists with biro pens writing down my reply to the Minister in their notebooks. A little African girl, dressed in white, offered me, with a bow, a small bunch of faded flowers. Then I climbed up the gangway of the plane, slowly, so as to allow the photographers to recapture my celebrated smile. But as I entered the plane I dropped my smile so abruptly that the hostess, who herself ought to have known all about false, mechanical smiles, was frightened and enquired whether perhaps I was not feeling well.

I shook my head and sat down, while the tears, irresistibly, gushed from my eyes and wetted my cheeks. I was conscious of a terrible distress, which I have felt now, almost always, for at least two years, and this distress, as usual, forced me to a timid, awkward exhibitionism. I could see the white trousers of a man sitting beside me; and that was enough to make me, in fastening my seat-belt, pull up slightly my already very short miniskirt so that my neighbour should see my splendid legs. There was one chance in a million that this man would not know who I was; one chance in a thousand million that he would be attractive to me; and I did not want to risk losing him. And so I exhibited my legs. If, on the other hand, he turned out to be one of the usual admirers and, into the bargain—as almost always—repellent, it would be easy for me to put him in his place with one of my celebrated, sarcastic retorts.

The aeroplane, after taxiing along the whole of the runway, came to a halt with its engines turning at full speed. I could not help looking at my neighbour's hand as it lay on the arm of the seat. It was the hand of a young man, large and strong, with a special kind of dark red colouring like that of blood, which I had never seen before. My distress, however, was stronger than my curiosity. I started crying again, looking at the illuminated notice at the far end of the plane: 'Fasten your seat-belts. No smoking.' Then the aeroplane started all of a sudden and, after a brief run, literally uprooted itself from the ground, rising in an almost vertical line towards the sky. As if I were frightened, I placed my hand on top of my neighbour's hand. The plane gave a violent shudder, of which I took advantage to squeeze his hand convulsively. Then I turned and looked at him.

I had not been mistaken: 'he' it was. Young, handsome, and certainly ignorant of who I was. Two things struck me in particular: the grey-green colour and the as it were liquid quality of his eyes, as though they had been deprived of sight and blinded by that same liquid quality; and the difference in colour between his very light complexion and his very dark hands. I looked at him and he looked at me. With two tears rolling down my cheeks I said, with a gasp, 'I feel so lonely.'

He answered me with a smile, displaying sharp, white teeth, like those of a wolf. 'A beautiful woman like you—lonely?'

'Lonely precisely because beautiful.'

'Strange. I thought beauty made encounters and friendships and love affairs easy.'

'Yes, but on condition that it stays outside the market.'

'What market?'

'The market in which beauty is offered as a piece of merchandise like any other.'

'And what then?'

'Then there cease to be any acquaintanceships or friendships or love affairs that demand the smallest degree of

choice, of freedom, of independence. There are merely the
high or low market quotations.'

'And your own beauty . . . Has that not stayed outside the
market?'

He asked the question in an ingenuous, unsuspecting tone
which could not have been simulated. He truly did not know
who I was. With a sigh, I said, 'No, my beauty has been on
the market for years. I'm a very well-known film actress,
famous, in fact. And my quotations are among the highest.'

'Oh, really?'

I had a suspicion that he was making fun of me. His wolf-
like smile, especially, and the ambiguous liquid look of his
eyes had something disturbing about them. I said firmly, 'I'm
called . . .' and gave him my name. Then, seeing that he remained completely unmoved, I added, 'Possibly you've never
heard my name?'

He replied with some embarrassment, 'I've been for some
years in an almost inaccessible region of Africa. I am an
explorer. For six years I've been living in a wild part of the
country, full of marshes and forests and climbing lianas and
wild beasts. No news reached me from the . . . from the outside world. But now, as soon as I get to Europe, I shall go
and see your films. But why are you crying?'

I shook my head, incapable of speech, but still tightly
squeezing his hand. Then I calmed down and said, 'Judge
for yourself. I was born in a little country town, of five thousand inhabitants. Take note of that five thousand. Five thousand people are quite a good number; but five thousand
inhabitants go to make up a small locality, one of those
places in which there is just one specimen of each thing:
one chemist's shop, one church, one stationer's and book-
shop, one café, one tobacconist's, one cinema and so on. At
fifteen I knew practically all of the five thousand inhabitants
of my little town and they knew me. If I went out walking
at sunset they all greeted me and I greeted them all. If I
went shopping, the shopkeepers called me by name and I
called the shopkeepers by name. If I went out of the town
to take a walk along the main road, I knew who the peasants
were working in the fields and they knew equally well who

I was. In fact I knew, and was known by, five thousand people in a direct, affectionate and physical way. When I say "physical" I mean that all these people had set eyes, at least once, not merely on my photograph but upon my actual person in flesh and blood. And I myself, in turn, had set eyes upon them. And now let us leap forward ten years. I am twenty-five, I am famous and, as I have told you, I feel more and more lonely. I am not a stupid woman, I know what's what, I never stop thinking about this solitude of mine, and finally it seems to me that it can be explained in this way. This solitude is due to a mistake on my part, to a—how can I explain it?—to an error of calculation. It is just as if, at the beginning of my triumphant career, I had said to myself, "If, when I was an obscure young girl in a country town, I knew and was affectionately and physically known by all the five thousand inhabitants, all the more reason why, when I am known to the whole world, I shall be known by, and shall know, affectionately and physically, millions and millions of people. This collective affection will warm my heart. Never, never again shall I feel lonely."'

'Instead of which . . .?'

'It was a mistake, as I have said. In reality to be celebrated means to be alone. Celebrity is like the glass in a shop window: you are put on show, everyone looks at you as they walk past on the pavement, but no one can touch you and you can touch no one. I mean actually *touch*, as I am touching your hand at this moment.'

He looked at me with sympathy—perhaps. But he said, 'It doesn't matter. You're famous.'

'D'you think it's so fine to be famous?'

'It's the finest thing in the world. I myself would do anything to be famous; I would even commit a crime.'

'You would be famous for one afternoon. With the second edition of the papers you would·vanish again into nothingness.'

'But what makes you think I should murder some ordinary person? I should murder a celebrated person. That person's celebrity would become mine, just as here in Africa it was once believed that by eating one's enemy's liver one would inherit his courage.'

Our conversation was interrupted because the aeroplane was starting to descend. All at once, as the plane touched the ground and bounced in the usual way with all its engines roaring, I realized that my neighbour had risen from his seat and preceded me towards the door. I saw him at the head of the queue of travellers who were already preparing to descend; there were twenty people between him and me and I was convinced that I should lose him. I had been alone before I met him, I had been with him little more than one hour, and now I should be alone again.

In the first-class hotel, in the capital of the new African republic I was about to visit, they gave me a suite: bedroom, sitting-room and bathroom. On the table stood a big basket full of tropical fruit, with a note which I did not open because I knew in advance what it would contain—the printed compliments of the management. I put on a dressing-gown, went over to the window and looked out. The window looked over the sea which, troubled and almost white, seemed to be boiling in the oppressive light, filling the darkened sky with mist. But right opposite the hotel, on the far side of the deserted promenade, was a poster as big as a cinema screen. Underneath the title, in large red letters, was my own name, and in a corner there was I, half naked in the arms of the leading man.

There was a knock at the door, I called, 'Come in', and then was in no way surprised to see that it was my neighbour from the aeroplane. He closed the door, came over to me and took me in his arms. But he did not kiss me. He drew back a little and said, 'I pretended not to know who you were. On the other hand I knew it all the time, I knew it perfectly well. A lot of magazines used to arrive at the clinic and I cut out your photographs and stuck them up on the walls of my room.'

'Why, what clinic? Aren't you an explorer, haven't you been living for six years in a region full of marshes and forests?'

'Yes, that was just what the doctor said to me too: you're

an explorer, you've been hidden away amongst the marshes and forests. You ought to get out.'

Suddenly I understood what was happening to me and, immediately afterwards, what had happened to me so far and what was going to happen to me. Was I frightened? Not really. But I pretended to be and, releasing myself from his arms with a cry of only moderate terror, I ran towards the door. I knew that it was locked and that he had put the key in his pocket. Nevertheless I made a pretence of battering against the door with my fists. I was an actress, after all, and as an actress I would die.

He fired the first shot at me as I was standing at the door. Then he put two or three or four more bullets into me. I left the door and went and lay down on the bed, so as to die in a decent manner. I knew I was losing a lot of blood and I closed my eyes. I opened them again almost at once and saw he was bending over me and gazing at me. I felt a need to say something affectionate to him before I died. Gasping, I murmured, 'Are you content, my dear boy? Tomorrow you'll be famous, yes, famous all over the world.'

PLURAL SINGULAR

I am a thoughtful woman, silent, and one who loves to listen. I do not allow my thoughts to become known; I keep them to myself. This is made easy for me by my round, smiling, pretty face. It is the face of a doll. Indeed, don't people sometimes say, of someone who does not allow thoughts and feelings to be seen, that she has a doll-like face?

Luckily I have a husband who likes talking quite as much as I like listening. My husband is what is commonly called an 'intellectual'. He does not write, however; for him writing would at once entail suspension of the incessant activity of his mind. And this activity is displayed in the following way. Any sort of particular and concrete fact or appearance is immediately seized upon by the little machine that he has in his head and is transformed into an abstract, general concept. In other words, the fact or appearance presents itself to him—and how could it be otherwise?—in the 'singular'; but when he speaks of it, he invariably speaks of it in the 'plural'. At once the fact or appearance loses all quality of concreteness; it becomes unreal. For instance, what can be more beautiful, in these days of summer rain, than the rainbow which, on some country road, when a ray of sunshine pierces the ragged grey clouds, rises, iridescent, from the thick vegetation of a broad green valley; while heavy rain is still falling, against the light; and branches laden with bright drops beat against the car-windows? But 'rainbows', in the plural, with their rules and characteristics, about which my husband speaks as soon as I draw his attention to this unique, particular, wonderful rainbow—what are they? Words, words, nothing but words.

One day my husband went off to work, just as usual. Being an intellectual, he had an intellectual's job : he was employed in an advertising agency. But, contrary to his usual habit, he came back home after not more than an hour. I too had started work (I translate from the German), when I saw him come in almost stealthily, with a worried, troubled expression on his face. I half-turned my armchair and asked him what had happened. My husband is small in stature, but with a fine head like that of a Renaissance *condottiere*: a large, straight nose, a haughty mouth, deep-set eyes. It is an energetic-looking mask; but, as I have already said, it merely conceals that little machine inside his head for transforming singular into plural. Now I was at once surprised that he did not answer my question immediately, as was his custom, with some long-winded generalization. I imagined that the thing which was upsetting him must really be something highly personal, and on that account so bristling with peculiarities of feeling that even his little stone-crushing machine was having difficulty in reducing it to abstract pulp. For a moment, in fact, as I watched him walking silently and furiously up and down the room. I hoped that, at last, for the first time since we had been living together, he would tell me the *thing*, just as it had happened to him, exuding all its uniqueness, its unmistakable, original quality.

So I waited quietly. Then, seeing that he did not speak, I left the revolving armchair and went and sat on the sofa. 'Goodness knows what has happened,' I was thinking; 'let us hope, let us hope that he will tell me the *thing*, in the singular. If he tells me in the "plural" this time, on my word of honour, I shall explode.'

Meanwhile, with these thoughts going through my head but with my usual doll-like expression, I followed him with my eyes as he walked up and down. And then, all of a sudden, he came to a halt in front of me and began, 'From the practical point of view, the professions are hypotheses of existence which require other people to confirm them. In competitive societies these hypotheses are always in danger of being contradicted...'

So there we were, back in the plural and the abstract. I was seized with sudden, violent exasperation. It was so strong that it no longer mattered to me in the least to learn what had happened to him. I opened my mouth and cried sarcastically, 'Blah, blah, blah!'

I have already said that my husband has a head like that

of a Renaissance *condottiere*, of the Colleoni type. Imagine, then, a Colleoni with his mouth gaping with astonishment. 'Why, what's the matter with you?' he said.

'The matter is that I don't know what has happened to you; but seeing that you start off with one of your usual general considerations, I'm not interested in knowing.'

'And why don't you want to know?'

'Because you never tell me the *thing*.'

'What thing?'

'The *thing*.'

'What d'you mean?'

'I mean the *particular*. You immediately enter into abstractions, into generalities.'

'It's my way of becoming aware of whatever it is that happens to me. Underneath the things that happen, one has to trace the laws that govern them.'

'Yes, but for some time now I've had a suspicion that you fabricate the laws in accordance with your own interests. If things go well with you, then things go well with the whole world. If things go badly with you, then things go badly with the whole world. It would be better to speak of the *thing* in a plain, unvarnished way, without extracting any laws or other general considerations from it. For instance, from the manner in which you began, I guessed that something had gone wrong with you this morning in, precisely, the field of your professional activities. Is it perhaps that you've lost an advertising contract? But never mind : if the same thing had gone right for you, you would have said precisely the opposite.'

'And what, in your opinion, ought I to do?'

'What you ought to do is to be conscious of the fact that you become aware of things according to your own interests, as indeed does everybody; you ought to leave generalities alone and simply report the *thing*.'

'According to you, then, I should become a kind of weathercock.'

'In a way, yes.'

The thing that had happened to him must indeed have been serious. For, all of a sudden, the little machine in his mind became jammed. He did not bring out any theory about women (I being a woman); nor yet about the duties of wives (I being his wife). No, he leant forward towards me, swelling with anger, and shouted, 'I forbid you to talk to me like that!'

At last! Here, finally, was something direct, precise, concrete. I intended to urge him forward along that road. I said coldly, 'I shall say what I think. You're a weathercock and, what's more, a very, very talkative one.'

Then, suddenly, he rushed at me. Our sitting-room, usually the witness of long harangues on his side and silent listening on mine, all at once saw a small man with a Colleoni-like head hurling himself at his doll of a wife and attempting to hit her. He succeeded, but not without an effort; and for a moment I felt almost a kind of relief: a blow, after all, is a blow: something particular, something concrete. But, immediately afterwards, anger got the better of me. I rose and ran towards my bedroom, crying, 'Everything is over between us.'

I took a suitcase and threw into it, higgledy-piggledy, the first things I could lay hands on. Then he came in, threw himself at my feet and embraced me round the knees, making me fall on my back on the bed. With a voice of genuine grief, he said, 'I got the sack an hour ago. I'm out of a job, and this is the moment you decide to leave me.'

And so, in the end, I had managed it. The mincing-machine had finally ground to a halt in face of my revolt; and he had told me the particular fact, intact, still undigested and not yet transformed into ideological sausage-meat. 'So you've got the sack?' I said.

'Yes.'

'In what way?'

'The boss called me in and announced that he was replacing me for lack of efficiency.'

'That's a precise fact, anyhow. Don't cry. You'll find another job. And don't worry, I won't leave you. You know what we'll do from now on?'

'What?'

'Whenever I realize that you're on the point of enunciating

some general theory or other, I shall say—but quietly and not in a nasty kind of way—"Blah, blah, blah".'

He gave a loud sniff, but was comforted and was no longer crying. I asked him, 'What sort of a man is your boss?'

'Just an ordinary man.'

'I'm sure he's not just an ordinary man. He must have . . . he must have some special characteristic.'

'Yes, he has a mole, a wart, in fact, just above his mouth. This morning, obviously, as he was shaving, he cut it. He was licking it continuously, without paying any regard to me.'

'Unpleasant, eh?'

'Moles, if cut, are very dangerous. They can lead to cancer. So one has to take care when one is shaving, because . . .'

'Blah, blah, blah.'

A GOOD DAUGHTER

I waited until my mother—or rather, the person whom, from the age of three, I had been accustomed to think of as my mother—had left the house in order to go to Mass; and then I jumped out of bed, went to the middle of the room and tore off my nightdress. The numerous mirrors round the room reflected my nudity with the tired, discreet gentleness characteristic of things that are old and of good quality. Thick, cut-glass mirrors framed in the doors of cupboards of a vague Louis Seize style, cream-coloured with linear gold borders. I could not help looking at myself. But not from exhibitionist self-satisfaction; rather from a new consciousness of my privileged lot that has for some time been an obsession with me. My body, indeed, young, healthy, robust and glossy, bears witness of my life as a girl who is rich or, as they say, an heiress; with holidays at the sea or in the mountains, foreign colleges, travelling, sport and, in fact, all the things that the majority of my contemporaries cannot afford. Things might have turned out differently; in fact, as I have recently discovered, they were fated to do so. I cannot yet manage to believe in my good fortune.

I went on into the bathroom, which was little less spacious than the bedroom. The bath itself was luxurious in the manner of thirty years ago, with a luxury so solid and so weighty that age had had no ill effect on, in fact had positively improved, the appearance of the massive tiles and the imposing taps. I stepped under the shower and was enveloped in the stinging torrent of water; it amused me to see how the water scarcely wetted me as it slid over my vigorous body as though over a marble statue. I leapt out from under the shower, wrapped myself in an ample garment of Turkish towelling and went back into the bedroom. Quickly I put on my plainest blouse and my shabbiest trousers. From the bedside table I took up my car-keys and went out.

Once I was in the street I was seized by my usual perplexity with regard to my car. I have a car of a very expensive make which can do two hundred kilometres an hour, and it is obvious from the bodywork that it cost some millions of lire. Last time I left it in a neighbouring street; but it was nevertheless a street in a quarter in which such cars are very rarely to be seen. True, I might go there by bus or taxi; but the first would take at least an hour, and the second—where should I find one to bring me back? I had an idea: I looked in at the porter's lodge of the building where I live. The porter was there, in his grey and red uniform, his braided cap on the table. 'Luigi,' I said to him, 'can you lend me your car, just for this morning? Mine, unfortunately, has something wrong with it.'

So off I went in the porter's cheap little car, in the direction of the quarter where Ada lived. On and on and on I went. I extricated myself with some difficulty from the town centre; I passed through the gate in the walls; I started off along an interminable suburban avenue. The apartment houses went on and on, one after another, all of them alike, enormous and crowded with windows. I noticed that although they had certainly been built during the same years as the house of my adoptive mother, unlike the latter they had not contrived to grow old but had remained 'new', even though they had a look of squalor and deterioration. Only things of the best quality, I reflected, know how to grow old; material of poor quality, cheap stuff, does not.

I parked the car in front of one of these big ugly barracks, passed through the huge entrance doorway and came out into the immense courtyard. Staircases A, B, C, D, E, F. I hurried through mangy flower-beds by little cement paths to staircase D; made a mechanical move as though to take a lift which didn't exist; ran two steps at a time up a staircase which was wide and therefore all the more squalid, and reached the second floor. There was Ada's door. Impatiently I rang.

The door was opened with the usual noteworthy precautions: the eye at the peep-hole, the door unfastened as far as the chain would allow, the questions in a low voice.

Then the door was opened completely; I was enveloped in a blast of stuffy air and the smell of cooking; and I threw myself into Ada's arms. As I pressed her to me and felt her big, soft breast against my chest and inhaled the smell of old horse-hair from her not very clean locks and placed my lips against her cold, withered cheeks, I wondered who could possibly have been the first to speak of the so-called 'call of the blood'. Call of the blood, my foot! We relaxed our embrace and I said, 'How are you, Mum?'—but with an effort, as I looked straight at her sensual, hypocritical, greedy face. With a sigh, she said, 'Well, what d'you expect?', but meanwhile she was looking carefully at my hands. Quickly I thrust into her palm the money that I held ready in my fist; and she put it in her pocket and went on, 'Ah, it can't be denied that you're a good daughter. I ought never to have given you away: you were the prettiest of the lot. But what could I do? I already had four children and besides, they were already growing up. But you were beautiful, beautiful, really beautiful. When you left, I cried for a whole day.'

Then she went off towards the kitchen, adding, 'I'll make you some coffee, a nice cup of good hot coffee.'

I went to a door well known to me and entered without knocking. A monumental bed, a double bed, blocked up the whole room, interrupting the view from the window. Between the window and the bed appeared the head of Giovanna as she sat in her wheelchair (she suffers from infantile paralysis) and looked out at what was going on in the courtyard. I walked round the bed. Giovanna has hair cut short like that of a page, a long, white, emaciated face, piercing eyes beneath thick black eyebrows. She looks like a rather fanatical, sinister knave of spades; but when she smiles, her smile is good-natured and she displays fine teeth, of a wolfish whiteness. Beside her chair she had a little table with the telephone on it; a book lay on her knees, which were wrapped in an old blanket. I made as though to speak; but she signed to me to keep quiet. I looked out of the window and understood. Right opposite, beyond the sill of an open window, I saw a man and a woman quarrelling. One could hear their distant voices; one could see their violent gestures which, precisely because they were violent, seemed nearer than their voices. Then the man put out his hand and seized the woman by the hair. The woman thrust him away and closed the window. Only then did Giovanna turn towards me. 'Every time,' she said, 'every time, at the critical moment, they close the window.'

'How are you?' I enquired.

'How am I? Just the same as the last time you saw me.'

'Well, it's two months since I've been here, I thought . . .'

'You thought I was better. No, no. One doesn't get better with this disease. At least, not in two months. Where have you been?'

'At Milan, with the grandparents.'

'The rich grandparents. Really it's a good idea: two mothers, two grandfathers and two grandmothers. Not at all bad.'

It was her usual tone and I was accustomed to it. I sat down beside her. She looked at me and then went on, 'But may we know why you come and see us? To see what a lucky escape you've had?'

I answered her in the same bantering tone. 'I don't know. Perhaps it's the call of the blood.'

'Aha, the call of the blood!'

The telephone rang. Giovanna lifted the receiver and spoke. On the telephone her voice changed: it was that of a concise, impassive secretary. She made an appointment, with the day and the time, and wrote it all down in a note-book; then she replaced the receiver. I asked her, 'Did many customers come yesterday?'

'A couple.'

'What sort of types were they?'

'Types from your part of the town, with money.'

'And what were the girls like?'

'One was attractive. The other, so-so.'

'And it's always you who answers?'

'Yes, it amuses me.'

'But where do they meet?'

'Here, in this room.'

'And how d'you manage then?'

'When they arrive, I go off, good as gold, into the kitchen, on my wheelchair. And there I wait until they've finished.'

I sat silent for a moment. Giovanna resumed, 'Would you like me to read you my last poem?'

'Yes.'

'It's long, I warn you.'

The telephone rang again. Giovanna took off the receiver and put it down without replying, sticking out her tongue like a mischievous urchin. Then she took some sheets of paper from the book on her knee and began reading in yet a third kind of voice. When she speaks, it is sarcastic, cutting; on the telephone it is impersonal, mechanical; now it was mournful and heart-broken. And yet there was nothing moving in the words of the poem. In effect it was a highly detailed description of the courtyard facing which she sits all day long.

I myself am a sporting kind of person and I understand nothing of poetry. And so, while Giovanna was reading, in a tearful voice, her poem, my mind wandered and I indulged in fancies. I imagined myself as an old woman who has had five children. Three of them have left home. The fourth is a paralytic. The fifth, the most beautiful, I have given away to a lady who has adopted her. I am old and poor and I contrive to manage fairly well only by arranging amorous meetings in my home. The daughter who for some time has ceased to be mine comes to see me. She is rich, she gives me presents, she gives me money. Oh yes, she is a good daughter, it cannot be denied, she is truly a good daughter.

LOVED BY THE CROWD

When I was a little girl, coquettishness grew inside me like one of those plants that take root inside a crack in a cornice and then, after some months, turn into a shrub and if you go to pull it out you discover that it has a root longer than itself. I was still a serious little girl in November, let us say, at the beginning of the school year; but by the month of June, when the holidays began, I was already so flirtatious that I myself was almost surprised at being so much inclined that way. In November I had been one of those cold, knowledgeable schoolchildren who seem like little old women; in June I was swaying my hips, thrusting out my chest, casting glances to right and left, laughing for no reason, placing my hand deliberately on my knee in order to show it off. But, above all, I was thinking about men. Or rather, I felt I was thinking about them: the thought was not present in my mind as a reflection, a calculation, a judgment; but there was the feeling that, whatever I was doing, that same thought never left me.

This is perhaps the moment for me to give a description of myself, partly because, by describing myself as I then was, I shall be able to provide a better understanding of the change that came over me later. Well, I was a girl of triumphant, resplendent beauty, and at the same time quiet, gentle and serene. My whole personality was bursting with a dense, eager vitality like a ripe fruit swollen with juice. I was aware of this vitality in the lustre and the movement of my hair, in the luminous dilation of my eyes, in the radiant meaninglessness of my smile, in the arrogant exuberance of my bosom, in the intoxication that rose to my brain at every step I took. I knew, of course, that I was beautiful; but I was not in the least conscious that I was continuously putting my beauty on show. I thought, for example, in all good faith, that I was merely following the fashion. Actually the shorter skirt, the deeper neckline, the more tightly-clinging dress were all my own.

Well, well, I was thinking about men and if fashion had decreed it, I would not have hesitated to go about naked; but at eighteen, I had still not given a kiss that was really a kiss. Strange to say, since I had been born into a traditional family and had been brought up with the object of matrimony in view, I did not desire to get married. My ambition, on the contrary, was—or at least so it seemed to me—to work. I wanted to work; and this desire to make myself socially useful concealed the desire to be attractive to men which was expressed in the movements of my body. The thought of work very soon became an obsession, as people say happens with the thought of sex. I took a diploma as a shorthand-typist, studied French and English, went to courses to qualify as an interpreter. Finally I succeeded in getting a job as a secretary, in an advertising agency.

I made a hit, as they say, at once. The director said to me one day, 'Susanna, you're a walking advertisement.' I asked innocently, 'For what sort of product?' 'For yourself,' he said. I did not altogether understand; I thought he was alluding to my coquettishness, which was all the time very marked, and I blushed. This director was a good-looking man, tall and robust, with only two defects: he was completely bald and so round-shouldered as to look almost like a hunchback. Naturally he fell in love with me, but in a gentle, respectful way in accordance with his character. I rejected his persistent advances; and one day, no longer knowing what to say to him, I came out with this explanation, 'I like you, Ettore, but no more than other people. If I were to love you, I should no longer have any reason not to love anybody.'

A short time afterwards, with the idea of pleasing me, the director put me on a poster advertising a new type of bathing-costume. Photographed in colour, I was standing in a simple upright position, with my arms and legs held slightly apart, against a white background. My chest and belly stuck out; my head was drawn back. The special point of the costume was that it was perforated over the breast and tightened over the stomach at the same time; so that all that was not clearly seen was set off by being placed in high relief. To put it briefly, it was an indecent poster; and in fact it had an enormous success. It was to be seen everywhere; and on the white background people wrote obscene remarks and rude words or made unmentionable drawings. Was I upset by the indecency of the poster and the vulgarities that people wrote and drew upon it? Yes and no. To put it plainly, the thing which had not yet happened to me in life had happened, instead, all at once, by means of that poster: I had, as they say, 'placed myself on the market'; and my offer had met with an immediate response. The scrawled remarks and the drawings were there to prove that a connexion had been established, that it had been a fortunate one and that it had been fulfilled to the uttermost. Moreover I knew that rude words and crudities had in them a potentiality of tenderness. In the remarks and drawings on my poster there was, precisely, this kind of tenderness.

But the poster, oddly enough, killed my coquettishness. I have often reflected on the fact that the two events were contemporaneous—the success of the poster and the death of my coquettishness. There was no doubt that there was a link between the two things; but it was hard to say what it was. Frenzied, eager, anxious to be attractive to men, all men, it had never occurred to me that I might be attractive not merely to those few men that I happened to meet in the street among the people I knew, but to the millions of males of an entire city. This was, in actual fact, what had now happened. That poster was, so to speak, a piece of 'mass' coquettishness; and it had aroused a 'mass' desire. But, contrary to what happens in a love affair between two individuals, this 'mass' desire did not develop in any way, it came to a stop with that one poster and with the one single season that the success of the poster lasted. My director, still trying to win me, put me on two further posters which were even more shameless than the first, if that was possible; but without any success. At the same time I became aware that my quality of coquettishness, by being transferred from my own person to the poster, had lost the unconscious character that had made it so disinterested and so intoxicating, like some giddy game. It had become simple, coarse flattery. It was perhaps for that reason that I now ceased to be flirtatious: I became diffident—something that, before the poster, had never happened to me. Or possibly, for some obscure reason, all my vitality had flowed out of my real body into my photographed body; and now, even if I had wanted it, I could not behave coquettishly as in the past.

Vaguely frightened by so many changes, I hastened finally to accept the advances of the director, for whom, in any case, I felt a sincere affection. The first time it was not a fiasco, but almost; I read, in his face, his disappointment at finding me so cold, so embarrassed, so distant. So different, in fact, from what I appeared. But he was fond of me and I was fond of him. So I left my family and went to live in a little two-roomed flat, in the neighbourhood of the agency offices. It was an empty flat; but, strangely, I did not succeed in furnishing it. All I did was to buy a camp-bed and a chair. There were built-in cupboards for clothes. I should have liked to put a table and a couple of chairs in the kitchen, but I did not do so. When I ate, I ate standing, plate in hand, at the window; or, more rarely, I brought in the chair that I kept in the bedroom and then, when I had finished eating, I put it back in its place.

I worked hard, the agency prospered, posters with pretty girls multiplied. The director, in spite of my absolute coldness, was more in love than ever and, apart from deserting his wife, would have done anything for me. As for myself, as I have already said, I felt an affection for him and perhaps also a physical enthusiasm; but I felt that our relations were becoming every day more and more reduced to the absolutely essential. In the office I no longer spoke to him except in monosyllables; at home, when he came to see me, I did not speak to him at all. But I listened to him, and indeed I even smiled at him. Then, however, there would come a moment when I took his coat, helped him to put it on and, kindly and gently, in a special way of my own, I would show him out of the door. This moment came sooner and sooner. In the end the director's visits lasted only a few minutes; and then, by common consent, they ceased altogether.

By now an irresistible force was urging me to cut all the links that held me to existence. After reducing and then abolishing all sex life, I gradually diminished my intake of food. Standing by the window, looking with a dreamy eye through the glass at the house opposite, I would eat a couple of forkfuls of spaghetti or a little boiled rice, more rarely a small piece of meat. But I hardly ever finished my meal; when I had eaten half the plateful, my stomach seemed to contract and I would throw away what was left of the food into the rubbish-bin. I never went out except to go to the agency; in the evenings I refused every kind of invitation for dinner or the theatre and stayed at home, all alone, watching television.

My life changed in the sense that it became further and further reduced; and it was the same with my figure. I had had what might almost be described as a full figure; now I was thin, flat, skinny. My face had become triangular, drawn, tight-stretched, my eyes large and dilated but with no look of tenderness, my mouth wide and covetous-looking but without sensuality. I was still beautiful; perhaps, according to modern taste, better-looking than before; but I felt dead. The director had taken another mistress, a girl who worked at the agency in the same room as myself. I accepted this and asked him whether he wished me to look for another job. Good-natured and still in love, he threw himself, weeping, at my feet, telling me that he loved me and that he would do anything provided that I would regain my love of life. I stayed.

One day I went by myself, in my little car, to the seaside. At a cross-road I came upon the famous poster with the bathing-costume, so I stopped the car and looked at myself. I felt I was looking at the poster with the same sort of nostalgia and regret as is felt by elderly women when they look at photographs of themselves when young. But I was not old, I was barely twenty-six. The poster was faded and scratched and torn. In one corner was written one of those coarse words which, as I have already said, can even be spoken with tenderness; and I caught myself murmuring, 'I only wish it was true!' Then I went on to the sea, to a not much frequented part of the beach. It was a fine day, with a blue, luminous, cloudless sky. But beneath that sky, thanks to the effluent from some factory or other, the sea was dark yellow with black stains in it. I was upset because, to be truthful, I had come to the seaside in order to die. I should have gone forward into the water until I could no longer touch ground and then I should have let myself drown. This would not have been a suicide, it would have been a return to life, from which, somehow or other, I had become detached. But in a sea like that, a return to life in the shape of death by drowning was not possible. I stayed for a long time looking at that yellow and black sea and then I went back into the city.

RAPED

I woke up with a start and felt immediately that the darkness all round me was foreign and unknown. A darkness that was different from the usual darkness of my awakenings, with a difference that was indefinable but certainly hostile. My heart was at once seized with anguish: why was I here, how had I come here? As though to find an answer to these questions, I put out my hand towards the centre of the bed and quickly withdrew it with horror: my fingers had encountered a bent back, they had become aware, through the crumpled material of a pair of pyjamas, of vertebrae, of muscles. There was no doubt of it, there was a man sleeping beside me; and I did not know who it was.

Finally I began to understand that, for some still unknown reason, I had been brought here against my will, by force. Raped, in fact. The fact that I was lying in bed beside a man with whom, in all probability, I had spent the night, justified the worst suppositions. Yes, two or more persons had seized me while I was walking along a little-frequented street, had bundled me into a car, tied me up, gagged me, transported me by night into this house, drugged me with some narcotic or other, undressed me, placed me on the bed and violated me. This reconstruction of what had happened to me struck me by its 'normality'. It is, in fact, normal for a young, good-looking woman to be subjected to this sort of violence. It might almost seem strange to me that it should not be so.

This, however, was not the moment for philosophical reflections; but, somehow or other, to get out of that apartment, take careful note of the address and then go forthwith to report my abductors to the police. I had been forcibly torn away from my habitual life, from my dear ones, from my favourite occupations, from my surroundings; the guilty men should pay dearly, very dearly. Thank heaven there were the laws, the magistrates, the police. It should not be permissible to subject a person to unspeakable cruelties without this conduct being followed by exemplary punishment.

As these thoughts went through my head I was gradually, in the meantime, extricating my right leg from the tangle of bed-clothes. I was careful to do this gently, without touching the man who was sleeping beside me. Then my foot brushed with disgust against a bedside rug that was no less foreign to me than the darkness which prevented my seeing it; I put my left foot, too, on the floor; I sat for a moment on the edge of the bed; then, with a single thrust, stood upright. I felt I was wearing a nightdress, but that gave me no clue: it was not my own nightdress; I noticed that this garment, too, was foreign and unknown. So foreign indeed that, with sudden violence, I tore it off me, pulling it away over my head. And it was in a state of complete nakedness that, having felt my way to the door, I opened it and left the room.

I found myself in a corridor that was quite ordinary and uninteresting, with four doors and, at the far end, the front door of the flat. A few little pictures, of the type that might be expected, on the walls, a stunted brass umbrella-stand, four mean-looking wall-lamps—all these endorsed the impression of strangeness combined, nevertheless, in a distressing way, with the feeling of *déjà vu*. And indeed how could it be otherwise? Criminals who rent a flat for their sinister undertakings certainly do not trouble to furnish it in an original, personal manner. Their object is not to live in it, that is, to create a familiar centre full of affections and interests; but to use it for committing their crimes with relative safety: and for this, one kind of furnishing is as good as another. All they have to do is to acquire some ordinary pieces of furniture at the first convenient shop: violence has always been naked and uncivilized, from the prehistoric cave to casual, anonymous apartments like this one.

It was very early, with dawn almost breaking; a grey light competed feebly with an equally grey darkness in the small sitting-room into which I now looked, advancing on tiptoe. I stopped in the doorway and peered into the room. I saw a sofa, two armchairs, a table, four ordinary chairs and a sideboard. Everything was horribly strange to me and, at the same time, horribly familiar. Again there was the feeling of *déjà vu*, or rather, of *déjà vécu*. For, without doubt, it had been in this little room that the least avowable and most criminal phase of my abduction had taken place. Witness to this, if nothing else, were some glasses and a liqueur bottle, some coffee-cups and ashtrays laden with cigarette stubs. On the floor was an empty cigarette-box. I recognized everything: cups, glasses, bottle, ashtrays, the box and, at the same time, I rejected it all.

I went to the window and, pressing my chest and stomach against the glass, looked out. I could have sworn it: the apartment was in a street which resembled it in the sense that it, like the apartment itself, was like a hundred, a thousand other streets. There, in fact, were the cars parked in herring-bone formation, close together, right under my eyes, and then, on the far side of the street, along the pavement opposite. There were the shops, still closed, with unlit windows, on the ground floor of the building facing me: the butcher's shop, the chemist's, the fashion shop. There were the balconies on the façade of the building; but I could not see the sky because, it seemed, I was on the first floor. The street-lamps were still alight, yellow in the grey air; in the middle of the asphalt there was a big hole, a bare, caved-in patch.

Shivering with cold, I left the window and went mechanically and curled up on the sofa, my legs drawn up against my chest, my arms round them, my face against my knees. I now realized that I should not be able to go and report my abductors, as had been my intention. And this, for the reason that, by transporting me to this anonymous house, in this anonymous street, far from everything that constituted my usual surroundings, they had in some way made me lose my sense of identity. Who was I? I no longer knew. I might be myself just as I might be somebody else. Now, if I were still myself, it was clear that I must rebel; but if, on the other hand, as I now seemed to understand, I had already become someone else, who could say that the situation in which I found myself was not a situation which had by now become normal for me and against which I had no right to rebel? Who, in fact, could say that my abductors had not already succeeded in fashioning for me a new personality that was more favourable to their own ends?

But what, in any case, were these ends? I nestled down more than ever into the little sofa, staring wide-eyed at the table covered with glasses, ashtrays, coffee-cups; and, all of a sudden, it crossed my mind that I must leave the sofa as soon as possible, put on a dressing-gown, go into the kitchen, fetch a tray, put the glasses and ashtrays and coffee-cups on the tray and go and wash the whole lot. Then I would have to open the refrigerator, pour some milk into a saucepan, place it on the stove, fill the coffee-pot, wait for it to boil, etc. Now how was I to reconcile these household jobs with the criminal violence of the previous evening? It was clear: the object of my abductors was to make of me an object to be made use of in every way, not merely in what we may call the 'physiological' way. In my own home, in my own surroundings, I was certainly a person with a name, a civil status, a profession; here I was no longer anything at all, or rather, I was what I was. But what was I? That was the point. In order to find out, I would have to know what my abductors thought I was. And in order to know this, I would have to do what they wished. Gradually, through what they made me do, I would at last understand who I was.

Suddenly, harsh and angry, a masculine voice called out the name of a woman, from the other room. The name was 'Luisa'. Since, according to all appearances, there was no one in the flat but we two, I myself and the man who had slept beside me, I had to conclude that the man's voice was calling me and that I was Luisa. Thus, then, a first point was made: for my abductors I was called Luisa. This Luisa, obviously, given the time of day and the situation, was being required to go back into the bedroom, open the shutters, announce that it was a fine (or a nasty) day, then go into the kitchen and busy herself with getting breakfast ready. Just as I had foreseen, just as was inevitable. And so, gradually, my new identity was being revealed. The old one I had mislaid and I should not find it again.

TWINS IN NEPAL

Two days before my wedding I was in my bedroom, with the dressmaker who was fitting my wedding-dress. The whole house was upside down. In one room there was the display of wedding presents: the china dinner service for twelve people, the silver spoons and forks, the radio and television sets, the ornaments. In another room was spread out my young bride's trousseau, produced entirely by one of the best dressmakers. Finally, in the sitting-room, my mother was once again telling relations and friends of the strange circumstances thanks to which I, daughter of the proprietor of a chain of draper's shops, had met and fallen in love with Attilio, himself the son of the proprietor of a chain of confectioners. The circumstances had indeed been strange. But I was content, in fact I was happy. Ever since my childhood I had been taught, both at home and at college, that matrimony meant happiness and, for the moment at any rate, I did not see any reason for not believing this.

Then, suddenly, just as I was holding out my arms, half-naked, to slip on the white silk undergarment, just at that moment my brother Francesco came in. You must know that he and I were twins and, at least in our case, it was true what they say about twins, that what one of them does the other does too, even to the point of falling ill, even to the point of dying. My brother had gone to Holland dressed like a young man of good family and with short hair; he had come back dressed in rags and with long hair. Since then he had not been living with the family but with a group of girls and boys like himself, in a flat in the neighbourhood of the Campo di Fiori. This, for me, was a great sorrow because, as I have said, twins suffer when they are not living together; and furthermore I had a profound admiration for Francesco and saw things only through his eyes, and he was, in fact, for me, like God on earth.

He came in, then, while I was slipping into my undergarment, and immediately poured out a torrent of nasty words at me: 'You silly bourgeois kid, you fatted goose, you slave!' Also he said, 'You're changing over from one chain to another', alluding to the chain of shops belonging to my father and to Attilio's. To tell the truth, taken unawares at a moment like that, I resented it and gave him a rude answer. And then he slapped me. And I returned the blow. He seized me by the hair and I did the same to him. Hitting and scratching one another, we rolled on the floor, under the eyes of the terrified dressmaker. Finally he ran off, banging the door behind him. And I collapsed into an armchair, in a desperate fit of tears.

How much it means, having a brother whom one admires and who, into the bargain, is a twin! All that day I was overcome with remorse for having answered him back rudely; and at the same time I felt that the happiness of marriage was like the gifts given you by mean relations who put an ugly doll into your arms and say, 'Pretty, isn't it?', and for the moment you convince yourself that the doll really is a pretty one and then, when you are alone, you realize that it's ugly and you throw it away. The fact remains that that same night I woke up with a start and, without thinking much about it, I put on a pair of trousers and a sweater, crept stealthily out of the house and went straight to the Campo di Fiori. I went up to the top floor of an old house where the door was ajar, went in the dark, into a series of little rooms that seemed to me to be full of beds, a veritable dormitory. At the side of a bed that seemed to be empty, I undressed and got in under the bed-clothes. But the bed was not empty and somebody at once embraced me. I wondered what Francesco would say if I resisted; I told myself that he would disapprove; so I did not resist but made love with my bed-companion. Then, still in darkness, he whispered, 'My name's Fabio; what's yours?' I might have replied that my name was Cecilia; but instead, I don't know why, I said, 'I'm Francesco's sister.' Thus began my life with the Campo di Fiori group.

I did not know why I had abandoned my family and my bridegroom; I did not know why I was living with the group.

But I was profoundly calm and serene and relaxed, because
I knew for certain that my brother knew, on my behalf, and
that was enough for me. So I found no reason to object when
Francesco announced that we were leaving for a country
called Nepal. I merely asked him whether he would inform
our parents and he replied very curtly that parents did not
exist. I was content with this answer and did not utter a
word.

Well then, it was November when we left and it was June
when we arrived in Nepal. Do not ask me what countries we
passed through in order to get there, because I did not ask
my brother and so today I would still not be able to name
them. All I have is a confused memory of having taken I
don't know how many trains, mail-vans, buses and even
carts. There were four of us, Francesco, Fabio, a certain
Giovanna and myself. Fabio and I were lovers; Giovanna
and Francesco were not.

In Nepal we went to Kathmandu which is the capital and
which lies in a flourishing, well-cultivated region reminiscent of Italy. Nepal also resembles Italy on account of
the large number of shrines, chapels, churches, convents and
other places dedicated to their Jesus who is called Buddha.
In the pale sky there are glimpses of the blue outlines of
gigantic snow-covered mountains. The town is small and
has little narrow streets with cobbled paving and gutters in
the middle of them, between houses of old brown wood, just
as in the Alps. Since we had hardly any money left, having
spent it during our journey, we did not go to an inn but
rented a room in the house of a Nepalese woman, in one of
those stony lanes. The husband of this woman worked as a
porter, going round all the time carrying heavy loads, wearing a jacket and nothing else except a cord passing between
his bare buttocks; and she, poor thing, made shift with a few
little jobs and a couple of rooms to let. Rooms! Let us say
stables, rather. The house was like an Alpine hut, with big,
dark interlacing beams. Our room had an earthen floor;
there was no furniture and one slept on straw.

We began to lead the life of pilgrims, going round with a
bowl begging for alms; and then eating whatever there was,

squatting on the ground in the sun, against the wall of a convent. But few people gave us alms because Nepal was full of so many others like us, causing competition; and so we had to do the best we could with necklaces and bracelets, or by doing some service or other for tourists. Meanwhile, partly because I was having little to eat and felt, as it were, stunned with weakness; and partly because, during the journey, I had trained myself to be subjected to the will of my brother, I was more and more indifferent to what was happening to me and to what I was becoming. What was I becoming? Sometimes, with a supreme effort, I tried to understand things and then I saw myself as I was. I saw my hair tangled and dirty, my face smeared with filth, my hands with black-rimmed nails, my feet encrusted with mud. I was aware also that I stank, with my clothes by now reduced to rags and my body that I never washed. One day I bent over a marble basin in which, among lotus leaves and flowers, a statue of Buddha lay on its back; I saw myself in the water and, to tell the truth, I barely recognized myself. I was a different person; or perhaps, more probably, I was no longer anybody. On another occasion I was leaning against the balustrade of a temple, bowl in hand, and I heard what a group of well-dressed, elegant Italian tourists were saying about me: 'Poor thing. She wouldn't really be ugly. But what filth! And did you notice how she stank?' Then I put out my tongue; and they went away.

Our money was finished and one day Francesco said, as if it were a quite natural thing, that the only resource now left to us was we two women, Giovanna and I; and so we two must make the best of it and look for men who would pay us, otherwise we should die of hunger, all four of us. We discussed the matter; I myself, of course, supported Francesco; but Fabio and Giovanna would have nothing to do with it and brought up the question of morality just as though we were still in Italy and all that had happened had not happened at all. In the end Fabio and Giovanna said they would leave us and go away, and they left and we remained; and next day I did what Francesco wanted me to do. Some people may say that it was not a right thing to do, that he should go round looking for men for me and that I should receive them. But you have to find yourself in conditions like that before you can pass judgment. And I do not mean merely poverty and hunger; I mean, above all, the state of mind to which I had surrendered, that of complete submission to my brother's will, all the more so when he made such an extraordinary demand upon me. For everyone is entitled to ask for normal things; and I recognized Francesco precisely by the fact that he asked of me something that no one else in his place would have had the courage to ask.

We went on in this new manner for about two months, and then one evening Francesco came in late, when I was already asleep, and said to me hurriedly, 'Get up, we're leaving.'

He spoke quietly and so I did not suspect anything. 'Where are we going?' I asked.

'Away.'

'But it's after midnight.'

'We must be well away from the town before it's daylight.'

'But why?'

'Because, if we stay, they'll come and catch us.'

'Who?'

'Are you ready, then?'

He had risen to his feet and was standing near the door. I rose too, resigned, already, and docile. Then he did a strange thing: he opened the door, then closed it again and went and lay down on the pallet at the far end of the room. As he settled down, he said, 'Well, we've walked quite a long way. Now we can take a rest, as we're a very long way away from the town.'

I saw he imagined that he had gone out with me, that we had walked through the night and had found hospitality in another Nepalese house very similar to the one in which we were living; and all this in the space of the few seconds that he had been standing by the door. He was, in short, delirious; and I curled up beside him and took his hand and watched over him. He went on talking; in his delirium he thought he was running away with me and that someone was pursuing us and that the distance between us and our pursuer was getting steadily shorter, and finally he said, 'I believe we must part.' But I did not understand whether he was alluding to the flight of his delirium, or whether he was lucid and was aware that he was going to die. Strange to relate, during the whole night and the next morning it did not occur to me to look after him or to go and fetch a doctor. I was resigned, but not with the forced resignation that one feels in Europe in face of things that are inevitable, rather with the resignation of that part of the world which is more like a kind of choice. I thought, in fact, that, if Francesco died, this meant that he wished to die and that he knew why he wished it, and I myself, as always, must not oppose his will. With these thoughts in my mind I fell asleep and so, practically speaking, Francesco died all alone, because I was sleeping and was not conscious of it.

After that, the rest does not matter. As it had been during Francesco's delirium, time flew, and it seemed to me that it was not almost two years that had passed, but only a few minutes, from the time when I had gone to live with the group; and thus I found myself again, just as before, in my home, with my family, in Rome. To make the time I had spent in Asia even more like a delirious dream, my fiancé Attilio actually reappeared. After all I had run away with my brother, not at all with a lover. My parents started talking again about marriage and I did not know what to do. Then one night Francesco came to me in a dream and told me that I ought to get married, since anyhow Attilio did not exist. It was certainly Francesco, only he could have said a thing like that to me. I awoke and understood that Francesco had not deserted me and I felt completely comforted.

REDISCOVERED

My husband left yesterday evening after a rather unpleasant argument. I told him that I would not go back to town with him because I wanted to stay on alone in the villa, for at least a week, in order to reflect on my life, to rediscover myself. And he replied that rediscovering oneself was a comic-strip commonplace; anyhow, it was all very well if said by a beautiful girl of twenty; but I was forty and the mother of a family and, in any case, what did I want to rediscover? I confess that privately I almost thought he was right. Yes, rediscovering oneself was a commonplace. Was it possible that, suffering as I had been suffering for some time, I could not manage to find a more original expression? But perhaps one of the reasons for my suffering was just that: that I did not know how to express it.

So I am alone, truly alone. The servant will come just for two hours in the morning, to do the cleaning. For shopping I shall go to the village near by; then I shall cook, I shall eat, I shall wash the dishes, all alone. What else? The rest of the time I shall use (here we are, back at the commonplace) to rediscover myself.

I sit in the entrance hall, book in hand. The sun, coming in through the big windows, casts a number of cross-shaped shadows, reminiscent of prison bars, on the wall, on the sofa and on the floor. It is a late September day that is too serene, too soft, too jaded. This softness imparts a feeling of unreality which, I surmise, is not altogether favourable to the rediscovery of oneself. I look up towards the windows: beyond the panes I can see the branches and leaves of a tree moving in the wind, but I hear no sound. All at once I am conscious that there is a complete silence, a silence of a special quality. It is a nocturnal silence, in other words a silence caused, one might say, by the suspension of life. It occurred to me that the sunlight, soft as it was, had about it a spectral quality, such as is usually associated with moonlight. Indeed the mild, golden splendour of the sun was reminiscent of the mild, silvery splendour, sometimes, of the full moon. Somebody once said to me that, according to the ancients, noonday was the hour for ghosts. I should not now be surprised if the ray of sunshine which is spread, like a soft shawl of light, over the armchair facing me, gradually assumed human form. The form, as it were, of someone sitting in front of me, with whom it would seem perfectly natural to hold a conversation.

Suddenly I realized that I was frightened. Not so much by the silence and desertedness of the villa as of the silence and desertedness inside myself. Very far, indeed, from the re-discovery of myself. I rose and went over to the french-window, opened it and went out into the garden. I looked at the English-type lawn with its incessantly twirling water-sprinklers. Big, dense shrubs starred with small white flowers grew here and there over this lawn. Then, in the silence, I heard a sharp sound, like the sound of shears. A branch projecting from one of these shrubs had been cut off and fell to the ground. And then a man in a sleeveless vest, bare-armed, became visible to me from the waist upwards, looking at me.

I went over to him. He was a rosy-faced young man with eyes of an intense, almost frenzied blue beneath a low, dark forehead like the peak of a cap. 'You—who may you be?' I asked him.

'The gardener.'

'This is the first time I've seen you.'

'During the summer I used to come very early, when you were still asleep.'

I was no longer frightened now. The desert was inhabited. A short time before there had been only the sunshine and the silence, in which I seemed to be an inanimate object like everything else. Now there were two of us; and suddenly, as though by enchantment, a situation had been created. It occurred to me that it was precisely a situation, of any kind, that I needed in order to rediscover myself. After all, what is it that novelists do? They create a situation by means of which one or more characters become manifested; that is, precisely, they rediscover themselves. The situation in which I had found myself for twenty years, with my husband and my children, had by now become sterile and no longer allowed me to manifest myself in any way. This was a new situation: I myself, alone; a young gardener; a deserted villa, in autumn. So I must pull myself together and make use of the situation to recognize myself, to rediscover myself.

Easier said than done. As I looked at the young man's face, my mind was a blank and all I could do was to ask him, 'What's the name of these bushes?'

He looked at me and said nothing. I plucked up courage and explained. 'What is the name of the bushes that make up this clump?'

'I don't know.'

'But aren't you the gardener?'

'Yes, I'm the gardener.'

'And you don't know the name of the bushes?'

'My job is to prune the bushes. That's all I know.'

'How old are you?'

'Eighteen.'

Suddenly I did not know what more to say. I made a sort of farewell gesture, turned my back on him and went back into the house. And there again was the spectral appearance, like the light of a full moon, with the soft, luminous sunshine casting cross-shaped shadows on the wall and on the sofa. A kind of panic came over me: it was not possible for me to go back and sit on the sofa, in that sunshine. It was necessary that, at all costs, I should find a way to clear the situation, to get it back into movement. I said to myself, 'That young man and I; I shall now do precisely the first thing that crosses my mind.'

The first thing that crossed my mind left me breathless, terrified. You must know that in the villa there is a cellar, completely dark and enclosed, which can only be approached by a small, massive door from the basement which contains the boiler of the central-heating system. Now the first thing I thought of was this, neither more nor less: to lure the young man into this cellar, shut him up there, double-locking the door, and then go back to town as though nothing had happened. The villa is isolated in the big garden which surrounds it. The holidaymakers had departed. The other villas were shut up, since it was autumn. The young man would not succeed in making himself heard. He would call out, he would shout in vain. In the end he would die in the dark, of starvation and terror. This, then, was the first thing that crossed my mind.

However I had bound myself by a pledge; and, though I was horrified at rediscovering myself to be so cruel and so sinister, I decided to face it. I went back into the garden, walking slowly and calmly. The young man was still there, up to his chest in the bush he was pruning. 'I have a rather heavy suitcase,' I said, 'which I want to put back in the cellar. Would you carry it down for me?'

'With pleasure.'

'Then come up in two minutes. In the meantime I'll go and close it.'

I walked quickly away and went back into the villa. I would fill any convenient suitcase with heavy things, books for instance, so as to make my pretext convincing. And, once I had shut the young man into the cellar, I would amuse myself by talking to him, through the door, of course. But then I would go away, without opening it. I felt cruel, determined, excited. For the first time for years I seemed to be living actively and with pleasure. I ran up the stairs two at a time and went into my bedroom. To my surprise the suitcase was already there, open and full. I had forgotten that I had packed it the evening before when I still thought I should be leaving that day with my husband.

This insignificant piece of forgetfulness sufficed to deflate me. It went to show that, in reality, my true, inevitable situation was that of a bourgeois mother of a family leaving for the town where her husband and children awaited her. To sum up, I had truly rediscovered myself and had found I was precisely what I was. If it were not so, I should have to accept the idea that I was a sadistic, gratuitous murderess. Better to consider this sudden outburst of cruelty as a proof, in reverse, of my innocuous normality.

I closed the suitcase, then went to place it by the door which, all of a sudden, with extreme slowness and hesitation, opened. It was the young man. I sighed and then, with an effort, said, 'I've changed my mind. I'm leaving. Will you please carry the suitcase down for me, to the car.'

He stood there with arms dangling, looking at me. 'A pity,' he said.

'Why a pity?'

'A pity you're going away. Such a beautiful lady!'

I myself, in turn, was looking at him. A dark flush had risen to his pink cheeks; his low brow seemed to be hiding his furtive, burning eyes. I almost burst out laughing. From all appearances it seemed that, unlike me, the young man had not taken long to rediscover himself in our delicate situation as mistress and servant left alone in an isolated villa. I said sharply, 'It's a pity I'm leaving because I'm a beautiful lady with whom some sort of an arrangement might be made—isn't that so? If, on the other hand, I was ugly, it wouldn't be a pity. Am I right?'

With a smile of brutal innocence, he agreed, 'Yes.'

'Well, I'm sorry, but brevity is the soul of wit. Take the suitcase and let's go.'

He did not move, nor did he speak. Then, addressing me for the first time with the familiar *tu*, he said, 'No, you're not going, you're staying here.'

'Come on, take that suitcase and don't talk nonsense.'

'Lie down on the bed.'

My heart was beating violently. I pretended to move towards the bed; he, in order to follow me, left the doorway; then I took to my heels. He seized hold of me as I passed; we struggled together; but instead of trying to reduce me to helplessness, he aimed, first and foremost, at giving vent to his feelings, and gave my breast a squeeze; I escaped him and ran out of the door, with him in pursuit. The narrow spiral staircase goes straight down all the way to the basement. I started twisting and turning headlong down the stairs.

We came to the low, bare basement room, with the central-heating boiler, a grey iron cylinder, in one corner.

There beside it was the cellar door. A ray of sunshine from the narrow window lay along the floor. I opened the cellar door, went in, turned the key and leant, panting, in the dark, against the wall. Then I heard the young man's voice saying, 'Come out. If necessary I'll even wait until tomorrow.'

'If I were you, I'd be thinking what you'll have to say to the police when they arrest you.'

'And what shall I have to say? I shall say that I've discovered myself.'

'Rediscovered.'

I waited a little, until I could breathe calmly, then, assuming an angry, proud, flattering expression, I put out my hand and opened the door.

ANOTHER LIFE

It was Sunday, my husband was out of Rome, the servant was having her day off and I was alone in the house. After all, I was not sorry. If for no other reason than that I could give myself up, without restraint and without shame, to the inexhaustible satisfaction aroused in me by my large and very fine new flat, in which we have been living for barely six months. I could still, so to speak, scarcely believe in this flat, the symbol of my rise in the world of my success. And so I went round from one room to another, stopping in the doorways in astonished, fascinated contemplation, even going so far as to touch the doors and the furniture and the walls with my hands, as though to convince myself that they were really there and that they were my own property. Yes indeed, I came a long way in ten years, from my parents' little flat—three rooms and a kitchen, in a working-class apartment house, staircase D, flat 16—to this luxurious penthouse; but if I had to say how I had done it, I should be embarrassed. Odd to relate, I have the impression that between the penthouse and the small flat there was nothing. The whole of me was here, at thirty years old, still young and good-looking, in the process of going round the rooms of my flat, on a Sunday. The whole of me was in the present, without background, without memories, here and today. Of course I had not reached the age of thirty without having previously been fifteen, twenty, twenty-five. Of course I had lived in other, more modest places before I came to this magnificent flat. What has happened to me is rather like the story in the Bible in which that woman was told not to turn and look back, otherwise she would be turned into a pillar of salt. Someone must have told me too that I must not turn and look back. And I have obeyed.

At this point my boxer dog started growling and barking in the hall. I went to the door and without opening it asked, 'Who is it?'

A woman's voice replied, 'Friends.'

'Friends—who?'

'It's Tilde.'

'I don't know anyone called Tilde.'

'Aren't you Graziella, then? I'm a friend of yours from ten years ago. Open the door and look at me; you'll see, you'll recognize me.'

I put up the chain, unfastened the door slightly and peeped out at a face I did not know. I was on the point of shutting the door again; but then the woman continued, 'Open the door, Monkey.'

You must know that I am tall, robust, well-made and even full-figured, but with a small head like that of a little monkey. My forehead is prominent, my eyes are brown and slanting, with a sad, sly expression in them, I have a small, snub nose and a full, protruding mouth. 'Monkey', however, is the nickname given to me only by my intimate friends, by my husband and parents. Certainly I did not know this Tilde; but she, it appeared, knew me. I took off the chain and opened the door. She came in quickly, looking all round. 'What a lovely flat!' she said. 'You've certainly done yourself well. Good for you! Where's the living-room?'

'This way.'

We went into the living-room and sat down on the sofa, at a good distance from one another, I at one end, she at the other. I was curious, perplexed, surprised: the more I looked at this Tilde, the less I recognized her. She must have been the same age as myself. But whereas I, from the handsome, exuberant girl that I had been, was now transformed into a sophisticated bourgeois married lady, she, on the other hand, had not, one guessed, changed into a different person; she had simply grown old, had deteriorated. She had dark bags under her blue eyes; her face, of a perfect oval shape, seemed to have become swollen round the small, withered, bitter mouth which in turn gave the impression of a bud which had never opened and which nevertheless had faded; even her nose was no longer what it must once have been: it should have been white, diaphanous; now it was rather red.

Finally I said to her, 'Let's use the familiar *tu* if you like.

But I don't know you. Honestly, seriously, I don't know you.'

'But, Monkey, I'm Til-de; don't you understand, Til-de.'

I looked at her, I examined her once again, conscientious-
ly. Finally I shook my head: 'Truly, I've never set eyes on
you.'

She was silent for a moment, watching me. Then, slowly,
she pronounced, 'Why, Monkey, is it possible? Now listen,
I'll remind you. We met eight years ago. You had been married for two years, but, in your own exact words, marriage
bored you and you had a longing for certain habits, for certain backgrounds. So you used to come to that flat whenever
Signora Elena telephoned you. And since I myself lived in
that flat we became, so to speak, friends.'

She was such a stranger to me, and so completely did I
not remember either her or the things she was describing,
that I could not help enquiring, with the greatest natural-
ness, 'A flat? Signora Elena? But what was it? A *maison de
rendez-vous?*'

Discreetly she corrected me: 'Well, not exactly, even if it
might appear to be. Signora Elena had a few friends. She
arranged meetings. I myself, however, was a model; you were
a lady customer.'

At this point she smiled; and then, suddenly, at the sight
of the two dark, ugly dimples that furrowed her cheeks, I
had the impression of something *déjà vu*. But let me be
quite clear. I knew for certain that I was seeing those
dimples for the first time; and yet they did not seem new
to me: it was rather like what happens in certain places
where one knows one has never been and which, nevertheless, one cannot help 'recognizing', so that in the end one
thinks one has been there in 'another life'. Yes, it must have
been precisely in another life that I had seen those dimples.
I continued my enquiry, in a detached, indifferent manner:
'According to you, then, we were a couple of call-girls—isn't
that so?'

'If you really want to put it like that—yes.'

I remained silent, making a final effort. Instead of looking
at her, I looked at myself, I looked into myself scrupulously,

earnestly, sincerely. But I found nothing, absolutely nothing. I said, nevertheless, 'And what is Signora Elena like?'

'Middle-aged, blonde, small, very short-sighted.'

'And where was the flat?'

'In Via Vicenza, in the neighbourhood of the station.'

'And ... what went on there?'

'Oh well, nothing special. Signora Elena did not like us to wait in the sitting-room. When someone rang at the door, she would go and open it herself; but first they would have to say the password. I remember the phrase: "I'm a friend of Giorgio's".'

'Who was Giorgio?'

'I don't know. Then Signora Elena would open the door, the customer would go into the sitting-room and Signora Elena would call us and introduce us. That was all.'

'D'you know why I'm asking you so many questions?'

'Why?'

'Because I'm trying to remember, I really am. But the more you talk the less I remember. I have never seen you, I have never seen Signora Elena, I have never seen the flat in Via Vicenza. Is that clear?'

Now it was Tilde who sat silent. With somewhat nervous movements she opened her bag, took out a cigarette and lit it. Then she said drily, 'But, after all, what does it matter to me if you don't remember? I've come to ask you for something and I know you won't refuse it to me.'

'For what?'

'A hundred.'

'A hundred what?'

'A hundred thousand lire.'

I continued to feel the easy, calm, imperturbable frankness of one who is talking of things that do not concern him. 'What is this? Blackmail?'

'Call it that if you like.'

'But I'm not giving you a hundred thousand lire. I've no reason for giving it you.'

'Yes of course, because you don't know me and don't remember. All right. Then it means I shall go to your husband. You had already been married for two years when you began to long for meetings at Signora Elena's. He won't be pleased if he comes to know of it.'

All of a sudden, to my astonishment, this surprising thought came into my mind: 'Not even blackmail, not even her threat that she will go and talk to my husband can compel me to admit to having been what I have not been. My husband will "perceive", he will not be able to help "perceiving" that I am not the person of whom she is speaking. That ought to be enough for me.'

I sat silent for a moment, then I said, quite simply, 'All right, go to my husband. Tell him whatever you like. I have no objection. But I'm not giving you the hundred thousand lire.'

Would you believe it? She looked at me, she examined me; then, suddenly, she too, it seemed, 'perceived' that I was not what she thought I was. For a moment she was at a loss, almost frightened. Then, in a vulgar sort of way, she resumed, 'Of course I understand, you've told your husband everything, you've got him to forgive you, I've come too late.'

She was silent; two tears of rage gushed forth on to the bags under her eyes, wetted them and made them glisten. This time I said nothing because, in truth, I had nothing to say. And then, behold, another change. Tilde looked from side to side and said, 'You are rich and I am poor. I've played the part of a blackmailer all for nothing. Will you at least lend me something?'

I fumbled in my trouser-pocket and took out the money my husband had given me for two days' housekeeping: thirty thousand lire. I gave them to her. We were now standing up, facing one another. Tilde hesitated, then threw her arms round my neck and kissed me on both cheeks in her emotion, stammering, 'You wouldn't recognize me, but it doesn't matter; it's been a pleasure to me to see you again and, more than anything, to find you in such good circumstances. You've done better than I have. Goodbye.'

I was left alone again. Deep in thought, I went to the door of the kitchen, opened it and went and stood, mechanically, at the window. The street, between its two rows of houses, was deserted, with the sunshine all on one side, where there were no parked cars; the shade on the other, where cars were closely lined up along the pavement. Then I saw Tilde come out of the main door of my building. Seen from above, she was, for some reason, even more clearly revealed as her true self: a woman no longer young, run down in health, exhausted, poor, vulgar. She walked away until she vanished; then I stood back again. My eye fell on a strip-cartoon magazine left behind on the window-sill by my maid. On the first page there was a story told by means of photographs with a title that struck me: 'The Return of the Past'. Then I recalled Tilde's dimples, which, a short time before, I thought I had seen 'in another life'. Then at last I understood. It was they, like Tilde, which had had a past and one could see it and they recalled it. On the other hand there are those, like myself, who have had another life and one cannot see it and they do not recall it.

EQUILIBRIUM

I woke up suddenly and, as though urged by some impulse which had penetrated through sleep to the point of awaking me, with a violent movement I turned on the lamp and immediately looked at my husband lying beside me. He was asleep, his head buried in his pillow, with one arm outside on the turned-down sheet. My husband has a brown face with fine, kindly features; but the arm resting on the turned-down sheet was a big, broad, muscular arm and I knew that this arm was joined to a body which was also massive and coarse. My husband is an adolescent with the body of a big man of forty; or, if you prefer, a big man of forty with the face of an adolescent. This contrast between the gentle head and the coarse body certainly has some significance, and for a short time I gazed spellbound at my sleeping husband, seeking to understand the significance of this contradiction in him. But I did not succeed in discovering it. Perhaps it means that I love his head and hate his body; or perhaps—who knows, everything is possible—it means just the opposite. In any case my husband, for me, is a problem, that much is certain. A problem so tormenting that it causes me to wake up suddenly in the night in order to look at him, as one looks at the total of a bill that is incorrect, even if the mistake is not visible and one does not know where it lies.

The problem of my husband is that I have given him everything, youth, beauty, intelligence (yes, even intelligence, for I was reading for a degree and for him I abandoned my studies)—everything, I repeat; and in exchange I have received nothing. Or rather, yes, I have; in exchange he gave me the job of assistant in his jeweller's shop. I have also given him two children, a boy and a girl, who are now nine and ten years old. It is perhaps on account of this child-bearing that I have become the shadow of myself. I had a well-rounded figure, and now I am bony. I had a face that was bursting with vitality, now my features are drawn as though I were perpetually hungry and thirsty. I am like a vine after the grape-harvest, when you can walk among the vine-branches and see nothing but withered, yellow leaves and not a single cluster of fruit. I belong, in fact, to that class of women with haunted faces and of imposing build of whom people say, with retrospective admiration, 'Ah yes, certainly in her time she must have been handsome.'

All this I was thinking as I continued looking at him while he slept; and I developed my thoughts further. I myself, then, had given him everything and he in exchange had given me nothing. Worse, he had made me into his shop-assistant. Thus I was in credit and he was in debit. The scales of the balance between us were not equalized: his, full and heavy, was down; mine, empty and light, was up. It was clear that I had to do something or other so that my side of the scales should, at the very least, be on a level with his.

I had an idea. But perhaps, rather than an idea, it was a physical impulse which, so to speak, anticipated the idea. I got out of bed, dressed in a great hurry, taking my clothes from the armchair on which I had placed them when I undressed the evening before. Then I put out the light and left the room on tiptoe. My husband had not noticed anything. In fact, as I paused for an instant in the doorway, I heard him suddenly start snoring loudly. I reached the front door, and then, outside the flat, the staircase.

We live in a suburban quarter, but the shop is in the centre of the town. At night these modern streets, consisting of blocks of flats laden with balconies, are nothing but a cemetery of cars parked in herring-bone lines. My own car was right in front of the main door. I got in and drove off at a high speed between those two comb-like formations of cars which gave me the feeling of death. The centre of Rome, luckily, is without organized parking-places. The buildings, unlike the cars, did not look dead, in the empty, silent night; but merely asleep.

I left the car in Piazza di Spagna and walked to the shop, which is in a neighbouring street. My plan for re-establishing equilibrium between my husband and myself was of the simplest kind: I would go into the shop, put the most valuable pieces of jewellery into a plastic bag and then go and throw the bag into the Tiber. My husband would have a loss of millions of lire; I would have proved to myself that I was not a mere shop-assistant; equilibrium would be established between us; and I would be able to love my husband once again, without romance, at least for a few years. As long as my sense of guilt lasted.

You must know that the shop has two entrances, one on the street, closed with a roller-shutter; and the other in the courtyard of the building. I preferred to make use of the latter. I opened the small door that was let into the main door, went into the courtyard of the ancient building and went towards a little door which leads into the room behind the shop and thus into the shop itself. I could already see, from a distance, that this little door was ajar, and I said to myself, 'D'you see? There's a thief and he's stealing things.' But this thought did not stop me. I pushed open the door and went in.

Immediately someone who was standing behind the door, his back against the wall, jumped out, gave me a push and made as if to escape. But then, in the same instinctive way as before when I got out of the double bed, I had a purely physical impulse. I barred the thief's way and then seized hold of something that he was pressing tightly to his chest with one hand, a bag which my fingers felt to be full of stolen jewellery. A fist struck me full in the face; but I did not let go. Another blow from a fist, on my mouth, served only to make me tighten my grip on the disputed bag with even more desperate strength. At the same time I gave a yell. I did not, let it be noted, cry, 'Stop thief!' as anyone might who is being robbed. Instead, I uttered a violent, inarticulate, bestial sound, like an animal defending its prey. This sound, it appeared, frightened the thief. He gave me a shove so violent that I fell to the floor. Then he rushed out through the open door.

For some time I stayed where I had fallen on the floor, in the dark. Blood filled my mouth; my forehead hurt me; but it was not that which prevented me from rising; it was rather—how can I explain it?—the feeling of astonishment

aroused by an unforeseen event. This astonishment, however, prevented me from understanding what it was that
astonished me. Then I made as though to raise my hand in
order to push back my hair which I felt was hanging over
my face. And then I realized that I could not move it: it was
keeping a convulsive grip, its fingers bent like claws, on the
bag of jewels which I was still clutching jealously against
my chest.

At last I understood. It was simple: I had come in order
to steal; I had wished to prove to myself that I was not, after
all, my husband's shop-assistant. Instead of which, I had
behaved just like a gallant shop-assistant who, when
attacked, had defended her employer's goods with her nails
A very different thing from re-establishing equilibrium!
The scales of the balance were now more unequal than ever.
I would have to postpone everything to some future time,
when I should have understood myself better. In the meantime I had to go on living.

I made up my mind; with an effort I rose to my feet; I
staggered into the shop and turned on the lights. There was
the counter behind which I sat every day, beautiful but
faded, displaying the goods to customers with unfeigned
scorn and detachment. I emptied the bag on to the glass top
of the counter: rings, brooches, bracelets, necklaces glittered
under my eyes in a brilliant, precious heap. Calmly, competently, carefully, I took the objects one by one and replaced them in the window where they had been. The thief
had also done his job calmly, competently and carefully. So
much so that I seemed actually to be the man himself as, by
some inexplicable change of heart, he restored the things to
their proper place after stealing them.

At last all was in order. I gave a last look round the shop:
no one could imagine that there had been a robbery there
a short time before. I turned off the light; then I left, making
my way through the back room and the courtyard, as I had
come. In the Piazza di Spagna I got into the car and started
off in a great hurry. I wanted to be home before my husband
woke up and became conscious of my absence. It was true,
I could have told him the truth. But what truth?

Unfortunately, as I undressed so as to get back into bed beside him, I dropped the bunch of keys on the floor. He woke up immediately and saw me standing there, although I was already in my nightdress. Without moving, he asked, in a tone of annoyance, 'What are you doing?'

'I had a nightmare,' I replied. 'I got up to get something to drink.'

'What sort of a nightmare?'

'I thought I was in the shop and that there was a thief there and I struggled with him and in the end I managed to make him run away.'

'Oh, you and your nightmares!'

That was all he said; he was already asleep again. I put out the light and went back to bed in the dark.

SUBURBANITE

I've miscalculated in every way and I've always known it;
but is there anything in life except miscalculations? Born
into a poor but snobbish family, instead of getting rid of
snobbery and accepting poverty, I rejected poverty and
devoted myself to snobbery. I had some excuse, anyhow,
owing to the atmosphere in my family. All I need say of my
father is that he acted as administrator to a Roman prince
and was as faithful and lachrymose as an ancient watchdog;
my mother, poor dear, longed to make friends with the
aristocratic ladies, even, it must be admitted, by means of
such improbable devices as asking by telephone for information about a servant-girl; as for my brother Piero, he was the
perfect product of such a situation, always, and in vain,
chasing heiresses with historic names. I was no less of a
snob than they, but I had the advantage over them of being
conscious of it. Of what use was this knowledge to me? That
is quickly said: absolutely none at all.

In my family we were always waiting for invitations that
did not materialize, for meetings that did not take place, for
friendships that did not consolidate. My mother had been
queueing up for years in front of the doors of drawing-rooms
hermetically sealed to her; my father had been blackmailed
when seeking admission to the same club as his employer,
the prince; my brother addressed his noble contemporaries
by the familiar *tu* and found himself answered with the
formal *lei*. We were, in short, a family which specialized
in stoically-borne loss of face, in bitter pills swallowed without batting an eyelid.

Piero and I had a singular relationship. Eaten up with
snobbery as we were, we nevertheless never spoke about it.
To make up for this, we gave one another mutual support,
by tacit agreement, in a loyal alliance. He would urge me
on, whenever he could; and I would do the same for him.
However, in spite of our efforts, we remained for ever in the

antechamber of real, genuine high society, in an expectation that threatened to be prolonged for the whole of our lives. Finally I had an inspiration: I must not besiege only the feet, but must aim at the head, of the fetish. At that time the recognized, undisputed leader of youthful high society was Edoardo, the mocking, indolent, fickle heir of a great family. I had never been introduced to him in a formal way, even though I met him everywhere; it seemed to me that he avoided me and this dubious situation was wearing me out. One night I awoke with a start and then, with the spontaneity of an action long premeditated, I seized the telephone and dialled my idol's number. Strange to say, I felt I was telephoning out of indignation towards him, as though he were someone who had tried one's patience to the utmost limit. I remember thinking, as I listened to the tone of the receiver, 'It's time it was brought to an end, yes, I've had enough.' I waited a long time and then, finally, a voice well known to me but irritated and fatigued, said, 'Please may I know who it is?'

'Someone who knows you very well but whom you avoid because you are frightened of her.'

'One of the usual suburban girls, I suppose. Where are you?'

'I'm in my nightdress.'

'What are you doing in your nightdress? You'll catch cold.'

'What do you say to my slipping my fur coat over my nightdress and coming to see you?'

'I should tell you to stay where you are. Who are you, anyhow?'

'I'll describe myself. Then you'll get an idea of what I'm like. I'm tall, with a small head, a long neck, broad shoulders, a very well-developed bosom, and a very slim waist. My legs are long and slender and come straight down from my stomach. I have round, black eyes, a broad nose, thick lips. My skin is dark.'

'You're a negress, then.'

'Well, well, at last you've understood.'

Goodness knows why I described myself in this way. Possibly because his definition of me as a 'suburbanite' had made me fear that that was what I really was. Whereas it seemed to me that the African exoticism, so much in fashion, would somehow or other escape any snobbish ostracism. But he, being a true superior snob who can see deep into the minds of inferior snobs, immediately unmasked me: 'Let's say, then, that you must be a black suburbanite.'

'Well, am I to come or not?'

He was silent for a moment, then he replied, 'Not tonight. Come tomorrow, but not here in Rome. Come to B.,' and he named a village in the Castelli Romani, 'tomorrow afternoon. You can't go wrong; our palazzo is in the village square. Go in, go upstairs, I'll be there expecting you.'

He flung down the telephone; and I, elated, went straight to my brother's bedroom. I went over to his bed, in the dark, and called him. He woke up and turned on the light. I told him all in one breath, 'I've just been telephoning to Edoardo and he's given me an appointment, in his palazzo at B.'

Although awakened from a deep sleep, although, as I have said, we had never confided in one another on the subject of snobbism, my brother at once understood what it was all about. He exclaimed joyfully, 'You telephoned Edoardo!'

'Yes, but I didn't tell him who I was. I passed myself off as a negress. Goodness knows if he believed it. Anyhow he gave me this appointment.'

We looked at each other in triumph. I went on, 'However, you'll have to lend me your car.'

'I'll drive you there myself.'

I went back to my room, lay down and went to sleep. But my sleep was restless and filled with nightmares. In the morning I felt ill; I took my temperature and saw that I was feverish. What a misfortune! I could have punched my head with rage. I called my brother and told him that for this time I would have to give up the trip to Edoardo's village. He at once protested violently, 'You absolutely must go. Even with a high temperature.'

'Yes, I *have* got a high temperature.'

'You must wrap up well and we'll take great care.'

So I resigned myself, reflecting that, after all, the fever would make my love-making more passionate—if love-making there was to be, as seemed probable. We drove those thirty kilometres in darkened air, in pouring, icy rain. I was trembling and my teeth were chattering from the fever; everything seemed to be happening in a sort of delirium. As we reached the village it stopped raining. There we found the palazzo, gloomy and smoke-blackened, with crooked walls and gratings over the big windows, in a deserted square of black, shiny cobbles, surrounded by a circle of miserable hovels. My brother and I entered a big courtyard with a long portico and made our way up the flight of stairs at the far end of the courtyard. The place had a strange look of abandonment and rusticity: there was straw and hens' excrement on the step; the window-shutters were loose and unbarred; sacks were piled up on the landings. We found the door of Edoardo's apartment half-open and went through into a vast and entirely empty antechamber. It was extremely cold, and the strangely livid light and a pool of water that had formed on the floor caused me to look upwards; and then, up there between the black beams of the ceiling, I saw the sky, grey and already reddening from the early winter sunset. A door opened and a woman appeared, asking us what we wanted. My brother mentioned Edoardo's name. The woman shook her head: 'He never comes here.'

'But it was here that he gave us an appointment.'

'He lives in Rome. The palazzo has never been repaired since it was bombed during the war. We live in one room, my husband and I and our children. The other rooms are like this anteroom: the rain comes in.'

We said good-bye to the woman who, mistrustful, did not even answer us; we went back into the square. My brother, without uttering a word, took the wheel and we left. Then, all of a sudden, I started laughing, with irresponsible, sobbing, hysterical laughter. I laughed for a long time and then I did not laugh any more; my brother did not open his mouth. At home, I went straight to the telephone and dialled Edoardo's number. I heard his drawling, contemptuous voice. I said to him, 'It was I who spoke to you yesterday.'

'Ah yes. The black suburban girl. How did your trip go off?'

'You're an idiot, a scoundrel and a degenerate.'

I saw my brother make a sign to me, in a nervous way, as if to advise me to be cautious; but I shrugged my shoulders. I went on, 'If you wished to make me see what sort of a person you are, you couldn't have done better. That ruined palazzo, empty and with the rain coming in—that's you all over.'

'How intolerant you are! One sees you must be an African.'

'I'm not an African, I'm a Roman.'

'Well, really! And what are you doing now?'

'I'm in bed, I've got a temperature.'

'Indeed! I'm very sorry. However, that needn't prevent you from slipping on your famous fur coat over your famous nightdress and coming here, to see me. Here in Rome, in my own flat.'

'Do you want me to come?'

'But of course. Why, d'you think I'm joking?'

'All right, then, I'll come at once.'

And so I did. Well, well, it's not enough to know that one makes miscalculations. What is needed, as I have already said, is to have something in one's life that goes beyond miscalculations.

LET'S PLAY A GAME

Filled with a desperate, impotent rage, I sat in the living-room smoking cigarette after cigarette and watching my little girl Ginevra who, perfectly quiet, was playing on the carpet with her doll. I had been waiting for an hour, after having waited for half a day for this fateful hour to come; soon, all too soon, Rodolfo's presence would be transformed from a reasonable hypothesis into a crazy hope. The looking-glass opposite me reflected, meanwhile, an image of me as an anxious, distressed, worn-out woman: a strained face with haggard cheeks; sunken eyes in hollow, feverish sockets; a tortured mouth, sulkily pouting and at the same time twisted in perplexity. My body was a crouching skeleton, with the abrupt movements of a frantic puppet. It was the image of a woman fallen into disgrace because she is devoid of grace. And what, in fact, is more graceless than a dog wagging its tail, whining and lolling at its master's feet? Well, this dog, alas, was myself. Take, for example, Rodolfo, and see how this wretched third-rate actor, stupid, fatuous and not even good-looking, led me by the nose and did with me just what he wished. It had been like that, in any case, from the very beginning. We were both of us in a bar, not knowing one another, looking at one another over our cups of coffee. Then I put down my empty cup on the counter and made as though to leave. Then he gave a whistle, yes, just one single whistle, as if he were whistling to a dog. And I, immediately, wagging my tail and whining, went back to lie at his feet. And that was how, with that whistle, our most unfortunate love affair began.

My other misfortune is that I am alone in the world. As a widow, I have no husband available to support me, however unfaithful I may be, and to make my lovers respect me. Nor have I any friends of either sex. I have only Ginevra, my little girl of seven.

Oh, children! Talk about children! Oh yes, let us unburden our minds on the subject of the gigantic, time-honoured fraud about children! Who, I wonder, was the first to discover that children are innocent? Whoever it may have been, it is obvious that he did not know them. Mark my words, *children are grown-ups*. Yes, they are grown-ups, but with the aggravating difficulty that they are children. That is to say, they are grown-ups inasmuch as they have the same feelings as grown-ups; but at the same time they escape the responsibilities of grown-ups with the excuse that their arms and legs, their bodies and heads, their physical being, in short, is not yet fully developed. And thus, while we 'feel' that, 'inside', they are like us, we cannot communicate with them, that is, we cannot talk to them seriously, we cannot confide in them, we cannot ask them for advice or help or assistance. And so, I should like to know what is the use of children and what is to be done with them.

At the present moment, for instance, if I could forget that Ginevra is only seven years old, I could at least unbosom myself to her of the anguish and rage aroused in me by Rodolfo's behaviour. I feel it would do me so much good to make her come and sit beside me; to have a drink with her—something strong, such as vodka or whisky—to loosen her tongue; to light cigarettes; even perhaps to open a nice box of chocolates; and then speak our minds in a truly confidential way. To tell her all about Rodolfo and myself. To go into all the details, make a minute examination of our two psychologies and show the differences between them, investigate thoroughly all the wrongs that Rodolfo has done me, and finally also deal with the delicate subject of his and my eroticism. The room would be filled with smoke; the bottle of vodka and the box of chocolates would be emptied; the time would pass; and in the end I should perhaps feel somewhat relieved.

But there could be none of that. Although I am sure that Ginevra knows all about me and Rodolfo, I have to go on acting the imbecile part of the dear little affectionate mother. 'No, Ginevra, don't pull your poor doll's legs like that. You're hurting her, you naughty girl; what would you say if your mummy pulled *your* legs in that way? But mummy loves you and would never do that...' etc.

Silly remarks, in which neither of us believes. But, when all is said and done, I am, alas, a good mother of the traditional type. And I do not feel inclined to forget that my child is a child.

These thoughts ran through my mind; I looked at the clock and saw that there was now no longer any hope that Rodolfo would come; and then, overcome with rage, I seized an alabaster ashtray and hurled it to the floor. The ashtray, of course, was broken to pieces. Ginevra lifted her head slightly and said quietly, 'Let's play a game, Mum.'

I looked at her. With her smooth fair hair, her white face and her blue eyes, Ginevra is the perfect Christmas-tree angel. All she needed was some candy-floss wings. 'What game, my treasure?' I asked.

'The game in which you're me and I'm you. I'm the mummy and you're Ginevra.'

'And then what happens, my love?'

'Then I shall tell you the things that you would say if I was grown-up like you; and you will say the things that you would say if you were little like me.'

So there we were: games. The great resource, the great fraud, the great sleight of hand practised by children. They say and do the things that grown-up people say and do; but as a game. You see the perversity, the hypocrisy, the dodge of 'passing the buck'? However I pretended to agree, 'That's fine, come on, let's play this game.'

Calmly, deliberately, she sat down in front of me and began in a falsetto voice that was supposed to be mine, 'Ginevra, will you tell me why you always get in the way when Rodolfo comes to see me?'

Of course! Ginevra was making use of the game to tell me the things I was thinking and hadn't the courage to say to her. I made a gesture of protest; but she stopped me, 'Remember that you're me, Ginevra. And answer my question.'

Then, speaking also in a falsetto voice, I said, 'Mummy, I get in your way because I love you and you're my mum.'

Cunningly she retorted, 'Nonsense! It's not true. You get

in the way because you're jealous of me, of your own mother, and you would like to take Rodolfo away from her and have him all to yourself.'

It was true, I was convinced that Ginevra, even though in a childish way, was infatuated with Rodolfo. But how had she managed to realize that I understood? Pretending to be disconcerted, I answered, 'But who ever said so?'

'*I* say so. On the other hand, what you don't see is that Rodolfo is kind to you and brings you presents so that you'll leave us in peace. Or else you pretend not to understand. Meanwhile Rodolfo and I are forced to lock ourselves up in my room.'

It was true, we lock the door: we have to! I, in turn, took advantage of the game to scold her. I said triumphantly, 'However, it's no use: I knock on your door the whole time with the poker. Or else I shout and yell and cry.'

She acknowledged that the thrust had got home, by her reply, 'You can do just what you like. You don't matter to me in the least.'

Faithful to my rôle, I groaned, 'Is it really true, then, Mum, that I don't matter to you?'

Viciously she answered, 'Not in the very least. What d'you imagine? If you mattered to me, I should certainly not make all that noise with Rodolfo at night, shouting rude words at him, throwing things at his head, chasing him even into *your* room in order to argue with him.'

She went on telling me bitter truths. I tried to defend myself: 'Yes, it's true. But it's also true that I've told you myself I would rather have scenes than be left alone in the house at night.'

She seemed to be reflecting. Then she exclaimed, 'Never mind, don't worry. Henceforth there will be no more scenes. Today I have finally become convinced that Rodolfo does not love me. And I've come to a decision.'

We looked at one another. My curiosity aroused, I enquired anxiously, 'What decision?'

Judiciously, according to programme, she replied, 'I have decided to kill myself. I'm going now into the bathroom; I shall take the little bottle of sleeping pills and swallow the lot.'

Frightened by her threatening clear-sightedness, I cried, 'No, Mum, don't do that, don't leave me alone.'

'No, I wish to do it and I shall do it.'

Swiftly she got down from the armchair and ran into the bathroom. I followed her. I saw her move a chair under the medicine cupboard, climb on to it, take hold of the phial of barbiturates. Then she stepped down from the chair, turned on a tap, filled a glass with water and emptied the phial into it. Then she explained, 'Now our game *changes*. You go back to being yourself; I go back to being *me*. Let's play a *real* game. And you must drink the pills.'

She said this in a quite straightforward way and put the glass into my hand.

QUARRELS IN THE RAIN

For some time now I have been noticing that, when dressing, I override the dictates of fashion, and instead of saying to myself, 'Now today I'll put on that dress which is so smart, with such a new, such a modern line, and which suits me so well'—instead of that I think, in a brutal sort of way, 'Now today I'll put on this blouse with a single button and this skirt which comes down barely below my hips. This will allow me to display my legs and my bosom, which are my two best points.' I am a widow, thirty-nine years old, it seems to me that I am still good-looking; and this impulse to exhibit myself would be legitimate if it were not, so to speak, so arrogant and frenzied. What is happening to me, in short? I am conscious of what I am doing but I cannot manage to control myself. This consciousness, which moreover is powerless and in fact cooperative—that is the novelty which I find disquieting and frightening.

Well, one day I was standing in front of the looking-glass studying with deep absorption, one of my usual exhibitionist rig-outs when I became aware of the iciness of a hostile gaze on my back. I turned round slowly and saw my daughter Tina, who was standing on the threshold and had been watching me for I don't know how long. 'Ah, it's you,' I said. 'You frightened me. What d'you want?'

She replied laconically, 'The car.'

'The car is for *my* use.'

'Then take me to the meeting. I'm late, and besides, the meeting is at Lucia's, in the country, and how can I afford a taxi?'

'I'm sorry, but I can't; I have things to do.'

Immediately, as though at a signal, she became violent. 'Come on, you haven't anything to do. Tell that to someone else, not to me. I know what it is you do, today and every day. You go out, you go off to Piazza di Spagna, you wander very slowly down Via Condotti and the streets near by, with your bag hung over your shoulder, pretending to look in the shop windows but really to get people to admire you and even to be accosted by imbeciles who also have nothing better to do. You might just as well go with me, especially as you behave badly to those imbeciles and then you come home again, as good as gold, like the good mother of a family that you are. Why, what's the good of it all?'

It was the truth; but it is not always pleasant to be told the truth. I answered sharply, 'All right, I'll take you provided you go and wait for me, wherever you like. I haven't finished yet.'

A few minutes later we left the house together. Tina was in needlecord trousers and a high-necked sweater that came right up to her ears. I noticed that, at the moment of getting into the car, she gave a severe glance at my abbreviated garments. I drove off in silence. Finally I asked, 'What is this meeting?'

'You know, Mum, why d'you ask?'

'About women, eh?'

'Yes, about women, if you don't mind.'

Decidedly I was irritating to her: but, as often happens in such cases, I was uncertain whether there was 'something' in me that irritated her, or whether it was I myself, my entire self, that got on her nerves. By now we were out in the country. The fields were swollen and green under a swollen, black sky. 'There's going to be a thunderstorm,' I said to Tina. 'How splendid they are, these spring thunderstorms! They give me a feeling of intoxication, of happiness, of spring, in fact. They make me want to go out singing in the rain, barefoot.'

She remarked ironically, 'That's the title of an old film, of the time when you were young, Mum.'

I but my lip. I believed I was being original, genuine, in my feeling, and perhaps I really was; but in order to express it I had brought out a commonplace remark and she had rubbed it in. And now the rain started. The first drops flattened themselves on the windscreen, forming for a moment transparent flowers with petals of water. But the sunshine persisted at the far side of the green fields over which the stormy wind blew long, livid, quivering furrows. I saw, between two pillars, a wide-open gate; I turned into it and went up the drive between two rows of oleanders which slapped the windows of the car with their rain-laden branches; then I stopped in the open space in front of the red façade—of the Roman farmhouse type—of Lucia's villa. Angrily I said, 'I've brought you here. Now what d'you want me to do?'

'Go to Piazza di Spagna, as usual.'

'No, I won't do that. I'm coming in with you. I want to hear what you say.'

'But they're things that can't possibly interest you.'

'Why? I'm a woman too, aren't I? Or else tell me you don't want me.'

She shrugged her shoulders and led me into the house. We went into the living-room, where there were sofas and arm-chairs arranged round the fireplace. Girls, all of them of Tina's age, were crammed together, ten to a sofa, four to an armchair. They made a little space for me, indifferently, almost without looking at me. They were listening intently to a minute little girl with brushed-back short hair, with a face that quivered all the time with tics and spasms, who was standing with her back to the fireplace and speaking in a slow, accentuated voice. I too started listening to her, at first for appearance's sake and then with reluctant and astonished attention. I had thought that they met together more or less in order to have a noisy entertainment; but I realized that, on the other hand, they were perfectly serious. Not merely was the girl saying things that seemed to me to be just; but they were the same things that I had been think-ing for a long time. And so, in the end, the difference be-tween these girls and myself was reduced, fundamentally, to this: I had been thinking of certain things all by myself, without mentioning them to anybody; whereas they had found themselves thinking of them collectively and had met to discuss them. The small girl was followed by two or three others: but I did not listen to them because I now felt a desire to speak myself. It was a frenzied, overwhelming desire, similar, in its irresistible quality, to that other desire which forced me, in spite of myself, to display my legs and my bosom.

All of a sudden I couldn't resist it any longer; I rose to my feet and, taking advantage of a moment when the place in front of the fireplace was unoccupied, I took the opportunity of going and standing there, facing the room. In a voice breaking with emotion I explained that I was Tina's mother and that I too wished to express my opinion. Not a murmur was heard: I mistook silence for consent, and I began. I thought I had not much to say; instead of which, it was as though I had turned on a tap: the words came pouring out of me in a way that was not only impetuous but also orderly, clear, convincing. The truth of it was that, without knowing it, I had been waiting for the first opportunity of revealing my thoughts; the opportunity had come and I did in fact express myself with felicity, with force, with precision. I was so pleased to be speaking and to be listened to that, as I spoke, it occurred to me that perhaps I had at last found the right road: from henceforth I would devote myself to the cause of women's liberation; it might even be that I should become one of the exponents most in the public eye: it does happen that the most genuine vocations have, as in this case, chance beginnings. But these conjectures prevented me from noticing that in reality I was being listened to in an icy silence. Then, all of a sudden, as I paused to take breath, a loud voice remarked, 'What a lot of nonsense!'

I answered with vehemence, 'These are my ideas, and I have a right to express them.'

'No one has the right to talk nonsense.'

'It's you who are talking nonsense.'

'In the first place, use the *tu* form. What's this formal *lei* for?'

'It's you who are talking nonsense.'

Now they were all abusing me, 'Shut up, stop it, go away, get out!' I looked at Tina: she was sitting with her head lowered, pretending to take notes. Suddenly I became calm. 'I realize,' I said, 'that what counts for you is not ideas but age. We belong to two different generations, that's all. I ought to have thought of it. I'm going.'

Once I was outside in the drive I again felt like my usual self, a woman circumscribed by family life, ruminating, all alone, on her own thoughts without finding anyone to whom to communicate them. I got into the car and started the engine. It was still raining hard, but less violently, with sunshine from somewhere or other lighting up the rain and showing it falling diagonally. I drove at a moderate speed down the drive, then, as I reached the gate, by mistake I pressed my foot on the accelerator instead of the brake. To my dismay the car gave a leap forward, went out of my control and struck the side of a car which was passing along the road at that moment. I had time to see that the driver was a young man with long, light-brown hair and a kindly profile; and to visualize, incorrigibly, the sentimental relationship that might originate there and then, in the rain, from this accident. I also had time—I confess it with shame —to recall the commonplace remark I had made to my daughter, about walking along singing in the spring rain; and to imagine that I would like to do this with him. Then, feeling well-disposed and almost pleased, I got out of the car and came face to face with him. 'Idiot!' he shouted at me.

'It's you that's the idiot!'

'Call me *lei*. What's this familiar *tu* for?'

So we started quarrelling, with the rain falling on us, warm and heavy, as if from a basin with holes in it. My blouse was soaking wet and sticking to my chest; but this nudity, transparently visible, had no effect upon him. In spite of his handsome face, he was just a middle-class man furiously angry at the denting of his special model. No walking and singing together—far from it! Suddenly I shouted at him, 'Shut up, you ought to be ashamed of yourself; don't you see we're quarrelling in the rain?'

Disconcerted, he opened his eyes wide: 'What has that to do with it?'

'In fact it has nothing to do with it. Now get away from the gate and stop a little further on. I'll give you all the information needed. I am insured, of course.'

HONEYMOON

What an idea, a honeymoon! And in India, into the bargain! The land of maharajahs! Of tigers! Of gurus! Of curry! After the wedding ceremony, since the aeroplane did not leave until the evening, my husband and I went to the flat we had just acquired, in Via Flaminia, and settled down to wait in the bedroom, the only room that was furnished.

My husband was impatient and wanted to make love; but I repulsed him persistently and violently; then I locked myself up in the bathroom and, when he knocked on the door and told me he loved me, I answered him through the door in a hysterical voice, 'In India! In India! We'll make love in India.' So he knocked again and then, as though beside himself, he cried that he was going out to have a breath of air and would come back only when it was time for us to leave, in five hours' time.

After he had gone I waited for another ten minutes or so, then emerged from the bathroom, took up my travelling bag, left the flat and went down in the lift to the garage in the basement. There I put my bag into my car and drove away.

I did not know where to go; as I drove through the crowded streets I thought vaguely of going to Fregene, to some friends of mine. But, after I had come on to the Via Aurelia, I saw a green notice-board with the words 'Leonardo da Vinci Airport'. And then I said to myself, 'I'll go to the airport and get on to the first plane leaving for India.' It seemed to me perfectly right to leave for India. I would go there *precisely* because I had not wanted to go there. Yes, that was the way one had to act. One had to do things *precisely* because one did not wish to do them.

I reached the airport, looked at the illuminated timetable and saw that there was an American plane leaving for India in about twenty minutes' time. I went to the desk, showed my ticket and passport and then rushed along the corridors and arrived in time to thrust myself in amongst the travellers who were quietly filing through Exit No 6. Half an hour later the plane was already flying above the clouds, with the regular, low rhythm that is so like quiet breathing. Then I took a small phial of sleeping pills out of my bag and swallowed three large tablets. Almost at once I fell asleep.

I slept and slept and slept. It may be that during my sleep I got out of the plane at Athens and at Ankara; it may be that I had lunch or dinner; it may be that I smoked some cigarettes and even spoke to my neighbour, a small, dark, plump Indian. But owing to those very potent pills all this seemed to me a dream rather than a reality; and so, in the end, I had the impression of having been perpetually asleep —dreaming, however—all the time I was travelling.

Finally, all of a sudden, I awoke completely. The plane was filled with an intense, dazzling light as of early dawn. I took my powder-compact out of my handbag and looked at myself in the mirror. I could see signs of hysteria, of fear and of aggressiveness in my burning blue eyes and in my small, disdainful mouth. The hand that held the compact, with the wedding-ring on its finger, reminded me that I had been married a few hours before and that the marriage had not been consummated. I made myself up as best I could and then looked out of the window. Far down below could be seen a great lake, of a dark blue, almost black colour, surrounded by clear, bleak mountains. I noticed that the shores of this lake appeared to be deserted. I stopped one of the hostesses and asked her the name of the lake. Smiling, she said she did not know; smiling, she took a map of our flight from the pocket of the seat; still smiling, she informed me, after a long examination, 'It's Lake Van.' I thanked her, turned over in my seat and went off to sleep again.

Again I slept and slept and slept. In my sleep I got out of the plane at Teheran, at Bombay and at New Delhi, I ate another meal, I even conversed with my Indian neighbour and asked him the address of a good hotel at Calcutta, for the reservations had been made by my husband and I did not know the name of the hotel where he had been going to stay. The plane had begun to descend, with bouncing and bucking movements, then it landed and I, still sleeping all the time, did all the usual things; I got out of the plane, crossed the tarmac, walked through long corridors, with my bag, behind a file of other passengers. Everything was the same as in Europe, except for the heat, the heat of a blazing oven, and the smell, a pungent, sweetish stench, a mixture of putrefaction and cooking. I went out into the open space in front of the air terminal and thought for a moment that I was being sought for a crime and that a great many people knew of it and were there awaiting my arrival. A large number of very dark men with wrappings like white sheets passing between their thin legs and then thrown back over their shoulders hurled themselves upon me, running and arguing, trying to carry off my bag and to urge me in the direction of a row of taxis. I saw that there were some big green trees with red and black flowers. Then, at the moment of getting into the taxi, I saw that the black flowers were not flowers but crows. I fell back on the cushions of the taxi as half a dozen dark hands were outstretched spasmodically through the window; I gave the name of the hotel which my Indian neighbour in the plane had mentioned to me. The taxi moved off.

At Calcutta, however, there are evidently two hotels with that same name; or else the Indian in the plane, for some reason of his own, had wanted to play me a trick in doubtful taste. The fact remained that the taxi, almost at once, turned into a quarter of the most obviously working-class kind. One street succeeded another; and in the blinding, dusty light I could see rows and rows of houses that seemed to be leaning one against another to save them from falling down, houses that billowed outwards, that were sunken and bulging and overburdened with crooked balconies. A black and white crowd—the white of the sheets, the black of faces, arms and legs—jostled feverishly along these streets, scarcely giving way to allow the taxi to pass.

Finally we arrived at the hotel, a wretched, decrepit house, bulging and balcony-laden like the others. I went into a small entrance-hall almost in the dark; all round the walls I could see white garments and the whiteness of many eyes;

everything else was plunged in obscurity. I showed my passport at the reception-desk; from a wooden board a dark hand took down an iron key with a label on which a number was written in pen and ink; and then I followed a boy who carried my bag up a tottering, creaking wooden staircase.

Once in the bedroom, I looked all round me. The bed, oddly enough, was in the middle of the room, completely enveloped in a white and flimsy mosquito net. The furniture, dark as it was, appeared to be of mahogany, in the English style. The walls were coloured with a feebly glistening paint, leaden grey and peeling off here and there. I went to the window and looked out. I saw a very narrow lane, narrower than any Venetian alley-way. On my side there was a row of houses similar to the hotel, crooked and bulging; on the other, a red brick wall above which appeared the corrugated iron roofs of some industrial goods sheds. The lane was deserted, except for one man who was walking slowly along supporting himself with his hand against the wall. Like all the Indians I had seen in the streets, he had a very dark skin and was dressed in a sheet passing between his legs and thrown back over his shoulder, leaving his arms and legs bare. Right opposite me the man stopped and, after a moment's reflection, allowed himself to subside slowly to the ground. He put out his hand, cleaned the flagstones of the pavement with his palm, then lay down on his side with his face against the wall, as though he wanted to go to sleep. He remained motionless; perhaps he was asleep already. Then I myself went to bed, opening the mosquito net and lying down on top of the bed-clothes; and I too fell asleep.

I awoke four times and all four times went over to the window to look at the sleeping man. The first time he had not yet moved: he was on his side with his face against the wall. The second time, he had turned on to his other side, with his face towards the edge of the pavement. The third time he was lying on his back, stretched right out, one arm folded behind the back of his neck. This time I noticed that, just below the pavement, there was a stream of dirty water, an open drain, perhaps. But the fourth time I awoke and went to look, the man was lying on his back with his head thrown back. The whites of his eyes seemed to be looking at me, but in a different way from the whites of the eyes down below in the hall of the hotel. The latter had seemed alive; the former appeared devoid of expression, merely white. His hand was dangling beyond the edge of the pavement and the dirty water I had already noticed was flowing between its thin, parched fingers. I looked for a long time at the man; then a frighteningly thin, shaggy dog, of a dirty yellow, came along. It sniffed at the man, then lifted its leg and urinated on his face and went away. The man did not move. I thought, logically, that he had either fainted or was dead. A third possibility might be that he was drunk, but that seemed to me improbable because I had been told that Indians do not drink.

Without thinking very much about it, I closed my bag, went down to the ground floor, paid my bill and asked for a taxi. Not more than an hour later, I was back at the airport. The aeroplane for Rome left almost at once. Once we were above the clouds I shut my eyes and thought of my husband. By this time he would certainly be looking for me with friends or relations. A bright idea entered my head: 'I have had my honeymoon, after all. It's true, I had it alone; but what does that matter? Is it laid down that a honeymoon must be had by two people together?' Reassured, I again swallowed three sleeping pills and fell asleep immediately.

I slept and slept and slept. Sleeping, I got out at New Delhi, at Karachi, at Teheran, I had lunch, I talked to my neighbour, a dark, very thin, very tall Indian. Then my sleep came to an end. I opened my eyes. There was a blinding light; I looked out of the window and far down below saw a great lake of a blue that was almost black, surrounded by clear, bleak mountains. I called the hostess and asked her what that lake was called. Smiling, she said she did not know; smiling, she took a map of our flight from the pocket of the seat; still smiling she announced, after a careful examination, 'It's Lake Van.'

METALLIC

As secretary to the manager of a business of some importance (incidentally, its importance was indicated by the
luxuriousness of the office: close-carpeted floor, sofa and
armchairs in real leather, genuine paintings on the walls,
vases with real flowers, etc.) I knew perfectly well to what I
owed the position that I occupied there. Not so much to my
knowledge of languages (French and English), nor to my
culture (a degree in Literature with a thesis on Lorenzo the
Magnificent), nor yet to my very good manners (I had been
educated at a famous college for girls of good family); but
to the fact that—let me say so frankly—on the very same day
that I presented myself to the manager, I went to bed with
him.

This, however, does not mean that I am not and, above all,
do not feel myself to be, solely and exclusively his secretary.
Moreover, how did this come about? To tell the truth, it was
not he that asked me. When, as I stood in front of his desk,
after informing him of my capabilities, I concluded without
smiling, 'And finally, I also have a good appearance, as you
can see for yourself,' he confined himself to remarking, ironically perhaps, that I was in possession of a 'disturbing physique'. It was I myself who interpreted this ambiguous remark as an invitation to a relationship that was not merely
bureaucratic. Gazing at him fixedly and in silence, I raised
my long, beautiful, slender hand to my breast and started
freeing the single button of my bulging blouse from its
buttonhole. But why did I do this? That is the point. I did
it because I did not trust to my knowledge of languages, my
university degree, my good education; and I knew for certain that, when all was said and done, I should not be able
to stand out from amongst my many rivals—they also bi-
lingual, with university degrees and well educated—except
in that particular way.

Someone may make the objection, 'How, in fact, can you

contrive to consider yourself solely and exclusively a secretary seeing that you are also his mistress?' I reply to such an objection with perfect calm, 'I consider myself to be his secretary and only his secretary precisely because I am also his mistress, or rather, because I am his mistress in a particular way. And this is as follows: between myself and my businessman love-making is not distinguished in any way from the other occupations in the office. A contract is dictated to me; then I am asked to make love; immediately afterwards, as though nothing had happened, there we are back again, I at my desk, typing, and he walking up and down the room, dictating. That is not all: in the first place, during and after our lovemaking we never cease to address one another as *lei*. That is still not all: even in the moments of the greatest abandonment I call him *dottore* and he calls me *signorina*. Yes, love-making is part of our work; in fact it disappears, so to speak, into our work.' My imaginary interlocutor may then ask, 'But do you like all this?' And I explain, 'Certainly I like it, because I have a horror of intimacy. To me life is a professional affair and everything must be absorbed, incorporated into one's profession, transformed, that is, into something professional.'

Well, well, this long preamble was needed to explain my behaviour of the other day. It went like this. I was sitting, as usual, at my typewriter and he was walking about the room dictating to me, when all at once he looked at his watch, gave a slight cough and then invited me to go through into the little adjoining reception-room. You must know that the glance at the watch, the slight cough and the invitation to go into the reception-room were all tacitly agreed conventions between us two so as to avoid the vulgar familiarity of remarks such as, 'Go on in there and start getting undressed; I'll be with you in a minute.' And so, obediently, I finished typing the last word, rose to my feet, tidied my desk more or less, and then went into the other room. But, to my surprise, he did not follow me. Instead, as soon as I entered the room, I heard the key turn in the lock. So there I was, thrown unexpectedly outside the usual professional ritual, into a region that was to me both new and repugnant and caused by inexplicable intrigues and sentimental undertones.

For a moment I stood there in amazement; then I had an intuition. I took up from the table a paperknife as sharp as a dagger, slipped it into my pocket and went out into the corridor. At the far end of it, beyond the two rows of closed doors, the little red lamp suddenly came on, announcing the arrival of the lift. Then the lift came to a stop, the doors opened and a female figure appeared. I had time to examine her as she came towards me. She was a tall, well-formed girl with a long coat which swept the carpet of the corridor but which was open in front so as to reveal, at each step, her splendid legs, almost up to her groin. Her hair fell loose on her shoulders and, as she came nearer, I distinguished her face: large, dark, moist eyes, a rather large nose, a full mouth. I knew the significance of that unrefined face, that exuberant bosom, those well-displayed legs. And my feeling, even before that of hostility, was one of disgust. She was the type of woman that I am not, and that all my life I have striven not to be: intimate, sensual, fervent, physiological.

Now she was close in front of me. I faced her, asking who she was looking for. She gave the name of my manager. Quick as lightning, I pulled out my hand, armed with the paperknife, from my pocket, pointed it at her throat and at the same time seized her by the arm and forced her into the cloakroom close by. Once inside, I quickly locked the door, then turned back towards her, flung her back against the washbasin and, still pointing the paperknife at her throat, demanded, 'Now tell me the truth, have you come for the job of secretary?'

Frightened, she protested, 'But you—who are you? I don't know you.'

'Answer my question, and answer it truthfully, otherwise I'll kill you: have you come for the job of secretary?'

'But who *are* you?'

'I'm the secretary.'

I don't know why, but suddenly she was no longer afraid. In a voice that was almost sympathetic, she said, 'Don't worry, I haven't come for any job.'

'Then why have you come?'

'What does it matter to you?'

'Tell me, or else . . .'

'Put down that paperknife, first. Well, I can tell you: he and I love one another.'

I began to feel relieved. 'You love one another? But is that really true? How d'you come to know that he loves you?'

'He's been telling me so every day for two years.'

'For two years? And how does he tell you?'

'How does he tell me that he loves me? In all sorts of ways. In words, for one thing.'

'What kind of words?'

'For instance, "my love", "my treasure", "my life".'

'Even "my life"?'

'Certainly. Has nobody ever said that to you?'

'Don't bother about me. And are you sure he has not suggested that you should become his secretary?'

'I've already said: don't worry. As a matter of fact, he has never wanted me to come and see him at his office. Today is the first time. If you knew what a scene he made to me over the telephone!'

'Then why have you come?'

'You want to know everything, don't you? Well, I've come because I need money. That's why.'

My fears allayed, I now breathed freely. So then, he loved her; he called her my love, my treasure, my life; he did not want her to come to the office; he was keeping her. There was nothing professional in all this. Nothing that could suggest love-making as I myself understood it, this is, purged of any kind of intimacy, included and incorporated in work. 'And why do you need money?' I asked. 'Does he not give you any?'

Shamelessly she shrugged her shoulders. 'There's always need of money. For the baby, if nothing else.'

'Why, have you had a child by him?'

'Of course; does that surprise you?'

I now felt more than serene, I felt content. Not merely did they love one another, but they even had a child. What could be more intimate than maternity? 'It doesn't surprise me at all,' I replied. 'In fact it gives me pleasure.'

As I said this, I let her go. She drew herself up and asked, 'May I go now, or is there anything else you would like to know?'

I looked at her and said nothing. She looked back at me, then shrugged her shoulders and went out. As soon as I was alone, I went to the looking-glass and examined myself. I was struck by the mineral, the metallic quality of my beauty. My blonde, drawn-back hair formed a helmet as of thin rolled gold. In my white, smooth face the eyes, nose and mouth were sharply engraved as though in the wood of a mask. The blue of my eyes looked like that of a precious stone; the white of my teeth reminded one of ivory. What more is there to say? In a short time I should go back into the office, and under some pretext or other I should open the window and air the room. For I was sure that the girl would have left behind the vulgar, sharp, strong smell of which my nostrils had been conscious all the time I had been talking to her.

RED LINE, BLACK LINE

I am a woman who takes life seriously, but who, strange to relate, never knows which way to take it. And so, when in doubt, I decided finally to do, always, exactly the opposite of the things that I felt like doing. A spirit of contradiction, it may be thought. Yes, certainly; but of contradiction towards myself, or, if you like, towards the inert, passive, lazy part of myself. This fixed idea of contradicting myself very soon become obsessive to the point of hallucination. What else but a hallucination, in fact, was the red line that vibrated and lengthened between myself and my fiancé Cosimo while he was expounding his plan to me? And the voice that exhorted me, 'Jump over it, come on, jump, you idiot?'

Cosimo's plan was a simple one: to go and throw bombs during the demonstration against the American embassy. I, as a highly skilled driver, was merely asked to act as an accomplice, by waiting at the wheel of a car in a street near by. When Cosimo finished, I looked at him and was struck by the contrast between his plan and his own appearance as a young man of good family, with short hair, no beard, in a grey suit with a white shirt and a dark tie. His voice, too, with its soft, upper-class Roman accent, was not consistent with bombs. I felt afraid; and for that very reason I said, finally, 'All right, I agree.'

At the demonstration he was to be joined by another member of the movement. And I was astonished to see him, for he was the attendant from the petrol-pump below our flat, from whom, on frequent occasions, I bought my petrol. He was called Tito: he was a good-looking, blond young man; but simple as a loaf of bread. Cosimo seemed proud to introduce him to me. But I started to laugh and said I knew him very well indeed.

We went to the demonstration; as for me, they left me in a quiet street, under the walls, two steps from a police van which was also waiting. I gazed spellbound at the policemen chattering and smoking. I reflected that they and I myself were all there on account of the bombs, but they were there to prevent them being thrown while I was there to throw them. Then, all of a sudden, the policemen got back into the van which started off at a great speed. After a short time Cosimo and Tito threw themselves into the car and I, as agreed, sped off immediately. Cosimo, in his well-bred, upper-class voice, announced, 'We got our policeman at last.'

They had indeed done so; that is to say, as I learnt next morning from the newspapers, a policeman had been slightly wounded. I drove Cosimo home and then returned to my own home, stopping at Tito's petrol-pump where he had to go back to work. But when Tito, after he had provided me with petrol, leant his elbow on the window to give me my change, I saw the red line vibrating vividly between him and me. And I heard the voice saying, 'Don't you see how much better he is than Cosimo? Make up your mind; jump!' Again this time I felt a repugnance, particularly on account of the social difference. And just because I had this feeling, I said in a soft voice, 'Tomorrow is Sunday. The petrol-pump is closed. What are you doing tomorrow?'

Later I saw the red line again many times. It was between me and my father when I told him that I was going away to live on my own. It was between me and Cosimo when I told him about Tito. Finally it was between me and a young Scandinavian couple whom I had gone to see some time afterwards, together with Tito. She was a painter and an albino; he was also a painter and an albino. And with a splendid little boy with flaxen hair. They lived in a big studio as clean as a mirror and almost entirely empty. Colours and brushes were all laid out in order on a small shelf, and they too were as clean as if they had never been used. We sat on the floor, on the carpet, listening to records. When the husband handed me the little packet, already open, with the white powder in it, I again saw the red line stretching out, vibrating, between him and myself. The usual voice whispered, 'Come on, be brave, make up your mind.' The wife encouraged me, winking at me in the most cheerful way. It was precisely that winking eye, inhuman, cold and blue as a lump of ice, that frightened me. I wanted to overcome my fear and I put out my hand.

One evil gets rid of another. The drug got rid of Tito who, one day, felt himself *de trop* and went away. And now, owing to the drug, I had a longing, all the time, to fly. I felt a consuming desire to go to the window, undress and then climb up and stand on the window-sill. Down below in the street there would be an immense crowd looking up at me as I stood, stark naked, framed in the window. After I had exhibited myself thoroughly I would take flight. First of all I would circle round several times over the crowd, gliding like a seagull above a stormy sea. Then I would set off like an arrow, towards the horizon.

This idea of flying became an obsession; so that one day when I had drugged myself more than usual I jumped up from the sofa, undressed and went to the window. It so happened that for some time I had been pursued by the not disinterested attentions of a certain big girl with the legs of a footballer and the face of a prizefighter, whose name was Tosca. She was present when I undressed for my flight. To run after me, seize hold of me by the arms with a grip of iron, and transport me bodily back to the sofa, was the work of a moment. Then, as she bent over me and systematically slapped me, I saw the red line suddenly light up between myself and her. The voice said, 'Make up your mind. Better a woman like Tosca than the drug.' But I had a horror of Tosca; and it was precisely this horror that, all at once, forced me to throw myself sobbing into her arms.

Tosca subjugated me to the point where we dressed in an identical manner, with the same blouses, the same trousers, the same top-boots. She, tall and robust; I, small and fragile: we looked like a variety comedy duo. She had subjugated me; however, she had not really conquered me. It is true that I am a masochist; but there are limits to all things. Every time I tried to assert my independence, Tosca would repeat, with obtuse brutality, the scene which had marked the beginning of our connection: she would start slapping me; and I would throw my arms round her neck. Tosca, in short, never changed; and it was owing to this stupidity on her part that, on the day when Tito, the petrol-pump attendant, unexpectedly reappeared, I immediately agreed to go off with him.

Tito was no longer the simple young man that I had known two years earlier. Or rather, he had remained simple but his simplicity was now that of the criminal. His idea was that I, as at the time of the bombs, should wait in a car with the engine running. He himself, in the meantime, together with a friend of his, a man called Trapani, would plunder a jeweller's shop. Never had the red line interposed itself so vibrantly, so brilliantly between me and the thing I did not wish to do. The usual voice was saying to me, 'Jump! Make up your mind. You have done it before, why shouldn't you do it once more?' I was terribly frightened. If I had not been frightened I should have refused. Instead, I replied faintly, 'I agree.'

Everything then took place as in a new kind of ballet. At three in the afternoon, on a cold, calm day with few people in the streets, I stopped the car in front of the jeweller's shop. Tito and Trapani got out. Tito dealt the shopwindow a violent blow with the jack. The glass was shattered into a number of sharp pieces that slid to the ground. Trapani thrust his arm through the hole, snatched some objects, threw them into a plastic bag and then put out his arms again. Just at that moment the car-engine, which I had kept running, stalled.

I tried to re-start it: nothing. It turned idly, with an impotent growl. Then I looked up and saw two policemen running up the street and coming towards us. All of a sudden I saw a line between myself and the policemen; but now, for the first time, it was black. I put my head out and shouted to Tito and Trapani, 'Get away, the car won't start.' I saw them run away up the street, scattering a number of little gold objects on the clean grey stones of the pavement as they fled. When the policemen drew near the car, I looked out of the window and shouted again, 'Are you after the thieves? They've taken shelter in that big doorway.' The policemen continued their pursuit. At the same time, the car-engine started up again. I drove the car back to the place where we had stolen it. Then I took a taxi and went back to my father's house, after an absence of two years.

Since that day I have seen only the black line. It was between me and my home, when I went in. It was between me and my father and mother, when I embraced them. It was between me and Cosimo, when he came to see me and after he had said to me that we both had many things to forgive one another, and informed me, foolishly, that he had discovered that he was 'reactionary, conservative and conventional'. Why then should we not get married? Strange to say, when confronted with the black line and at the same moment the usual voice bidding me to make up my mind, I had exactly the same feeling of extreme repugnance that I had had when Cosimo had told me of the bombs. And for precisely that reason I agreed to marry him.

How many cardinals were there at my wedding ceremony? I should say at least a dozen. I seemed to be stooping and kissing old, beringed hands all the time. Red skull-caps floated among the many heads of the guests, like so many flowers in a tropical marsh. Cosimo went round telling everybody that he had discovered he was reactionary, conservative and conventional; and I was all the time jumping over black lines, all of which were repugnant to me and it was for that precise reason that I jumped over them.

Now we are married and we have two children. Cosimo does not work: he administers his property and I mine. And he sleeps. Oh, how that man sleeps! Eight hours, at least, at night; and then a siesta of two or even three hours during the day. Sometimes I raise myself on my elbow and look at him while he sleeps. And would you believe it? The red line, the old red line of revolt, has come back to stretch and vibrate between me and him. Unless it is that I don't know how to interpret it. The voice says to me, 'Make up your mind'; but it does not tell me how to do so. What should I do? Take a candlestick and hit him over the head with it? Or else, more simply, go away on tiptoe and never come back? Or again, more desperately, wake him up with a sharp, piercing shriek, the shriek of my own seriousness and of my continual commitment both of which are always betrayed? Furthermore, why must the whole of life be a transgression? Or else the transgression of transgression?

DROP-OUT

Originally my home was an elegant and not very large flat in the Parioli district: two bedrooms, a living-room and the so-called 'service' rooms. A flat for a family of three persons, at the most. My parents slept in one room, I in the other. The servant had a cubby-hole of her own. The living-room, indeed, as happens in bourgeois families, was more symbolic than anything else, because it did not serve any purpose at all, not even for the consuming of meals, for we ate in the kitchen.

Then my grandmother died and we took my grandfather into the house; he too, like my father, was a civil servant, but now on a pension. We took him in because he was an invalid and his pension was not sufficient to pay for a male nurse. My mother dismissed the servant and took on a daily help. I was moved into the cubbyhole. My grandfather took over my room.

Then the husband of one of my maternal aunts, a master in a secondary school, was killed in a street accident. Left alone with a daughter of my age and with very little money, my aunt came to an agreement with my parents to come and live with us. A further change. My grandfather was moved into the cubby-hole. My aunt and her daughter took over the room which had once been mine and then my grandfather's. I ended up on a sofa in the living-room.

But soon, from Libya where they had been settled for many years, there descended upon us a brother of my father's and his wife, both of them chemists. In the interval before their chemists' shop could open, we contrived to house them as well, since they were exiles and without means. Another earthquake. My father and his brother slept in the same room, my mother, my uncle's wife and I accommodated ourselves as best we could in the living-room.

So now there were eight of us in that flat for three. At night the flat became a dormitory; in the daytime there was the inconvenience of waiting for the bathroom; in the kit-chen, at mealtimes, there was no room to turn round. In order to solve the problem of living together, my relations made up their minds to ignore it. They pretended to them-selves and to the others that everything was normal, in accordance with their own decent, middle-class normality. They were kindly, correct, urbane, dignified, with the added aggravation of reassuring clichés and commonplaces occur-ring automatically in their conversation. Every now and then there was a sigh or two, but barely noticeable. To me, on the other hand, life at home had become irritating to the point of madness.

This feeling of intolerance could not be explained merely by the discomfort. In reality I am a very difficult person. My bad character was visible even in my physical appear-ance. Rather ugly, my face is that of a boy, in fact of a hooligan, with small green eyes blinking through the smoke of the cigarette which I hold perpetually between my thick lips; a nose with nostrils that curl as though in endless dis-gust; and thick hair, black and glossy, growing right down between my eyebrows and giving me a low, stubborn-look-ing forehead. I am shy, reserved, diffident and silent. But I am also stupidly, crazily explosive. Patiently I wait, check-ing myself for a long time and slyly accumulating my fury. Then, at the slightest opportunity, I flare up. Then I regret it and tell myself that I would have done better not to be patient and not to explode; but by then it is too late.

That was what happened at my home. Already I was not very fond of my parents because of their obstinate, bankrupt middle-class outlook; but after all they were my parents: there they were and I had to stick to them. But now I had to endure five other people of the same insufferable con-formist, Philistine type. Strange to say, their prejudices did not irritate me as long as they expressed them in words, be-cause I managed to detach myself and not to listen. But un-fortunately I did not succeed in not seeing and not watching. My attention fixed itself on their gestures, on their looks, on their smiles, on their manners, on their clothes, on their habits. Boiling with silent hatred, I gazed spellbound at a tie, at a spoon raised to a mouth in a certain way, at a hairdo of a certain type.

The minor incident that caused my fury to burst forth occurred one morning when, as usual, I was waiting for the bathroom to be free. Inside it was my cousin Liliana, an idiot who spent the day varnishing her nails, trying on clothes, sticking false eyelashes on her eyes. The door was open and she was spending an endless time in front of the looking-glass, ignoring me. A few words were exchanged and then I exploded. I jumped on her, seized her by the hair; we struggled together and then I managed to push her head into the lavatory bowl and to press the lever of the cistern. She was still screaming when, having stuffed a few things into a small suitcase, I rushed out of the flat, determined never to come back.

I knew where I was going. I had been thinking about it for some time and perhaps it was also for this reason that I exploded. I was going to Carmen's; she was a rich friend of mine who, some time before, had organized, in a large apartment in an old quarter of Rome, a kind of community which welcomed people like me who had run away from their families and who were unable to bear middle-class life. The apartment was in Via Monserrato, at the top of a shabby old house; Carmen had inherited it, and before Carmen it had been the administrative quarters of a Roman prince. The house had a dark entrance hall, a smelly staircase, landings encrusted with damp. Inside there was a succession of rooms; little rooms and big rooms. With rafters across the ceilings, walls with paler patches against which pieces of furniture had stood for half a century, floor-tiles which rocked under one's feet. No kitchen, no bathroom or shower, only one lavatory. Carmen, who had the complex that rich people develop and who wanted to live like a poor person, had scarcely cleaned up the apartment, merely removing the worst of the dirt; and, apart from a certain number of camp-beds and straw-seated chairs and some stoves, she had not even furnished it.

She too had run away from home although she had not had, like me, the problem of overcrowding, and she had decided, as she constantly repeated to me, never to fall back again into the trap of the 'consumer' society. A strange type, Carmen, now that I think of her again! With me, revolt could be read in my face. She, on the other hand, gentle, serene, indolent, round and plump—nobody would have thought her a rebel. Yet there she was, huddled on a ragged sofa, ragged herself, at one end of a big, squalid room, absorbed in listening all day to her favourite records.

And so I began living in Carmen's community. Who else was there? There were foreign couples, from the north, with children even, in search of cheap sunshine. There were boys and girls of our own country who had fled from the provinces. There were two or three negroes who did not feel like living in the United States. There were some South American revolutionaries, Greeks and Spaniards. All these people slept on the camp-beds, ate their meals in snack-bars or hikers' restaurants, met together now in one of the big rooms, now in another, to listen to music or have discussions or just smoke in silence. I slept in the same room as Carmen and three young men who, however, were never the same ones: they changed every two or three weeks. Around Carmen, who was very popular and much loved, there were always quantities of people. I myself, on the other hand, sulky-looking and shy, did not give away, nor seek, any confidences. For the most part I stayed on my camp-bed, reading and smoking. Or else I sat at a little table scribbling away at a literary thesis which had been commissioned from me by a lazy student.

In reality I did not at all like life in the community. I did not feel any liking for my camp-bed companions; in fact, some of their characteristics began to irritate me deeply. For example, their dirtiness. I am a fussy person; but it must be admitted that many of them were accompanied by a very, very strong smell, so much so that I often felt a need to throw open the window and air our room. For another example: intimacy. It had been decided, absolutely, that we must all of us be intimate, must be friends for life, through thick and thin. But all this was rushed through from the very beginning, as briskly as possible, with two or three formalities:

I'll address you as *tu* and you'll do the same to me; all that is yours is mine and *vice versa*; you kiss me and I'll kiss you. Intimacy, however, did not make any progress at all and I felt myself as alone as before, in fact worse than before, and they remained strangers to me even if they claimed no longer to be so. And for a final example, promiscuity. Of this last disadvantage of living together in a community I could see the result before my eyes: Carmen was six months' pregnant but it was not known by whom; perhaps even she herself did not know. It was this fact of promiscuity which in the end caused me to explode once again.

One night I awoke with the feeling that someone was slipping in under the bedclothes beside me. I gave a hard push; something fell on the floor; I lit the light; it was a young man, a newcomer from Latium, almost a peasant, to whom I had made the mistake of offering a cigarette the previous evening. Infuriated, I started abusing him in a loud voice; then I lost my head, jumped upon him as he still lay on the floor looking at me in astonishment, and then began punching and kicking him. By this time everyone was awake and shouting; the young man, terrified at my rage, tried to get away; Carmen got out of bed, took hold of me by the arm, trying to stop me, and meanwhile preached me a kind of topsy-turvy sermon, so to speak: why did I get so angry? Even if I had made love with him it would not have been so terrible; who did I think I was, etc. At these well-meaning exhortations, I don't know what came over me. I turned on her, flung her down on her camp-bed, placed myself astride on her stomach, at the risk of doing her harm, and started slapping her. It was the others who rescued her from me; she was so astonished that she did not even react. I took advantage of the confusion to put my few belongings into my suitcase and run away.

I found myself in the street. I walked as far as the Tiber, placed my suitcase on the ground, lit a cigarette and gazed for a long time, in the darkness of the night, at the flowing river which could be seen far down below, with the moving reflections of the lights. I did not think of anything at all, I would have liked to cry but I could not manage it. Gradually I grew calmer. Then I went to wait for the tram that goes to San Giovanni. I knew a certain person in that neighbourhood who would put me up for the night. Meanwhile, as I waited, I said to myself that hard times had come for people like myself, with tender hearts.

HAPPY!

Red, red, red, marvellous Roman autumn! As I came out of the house, the avenue in which we live looked entirely yellow or red. Yellow, the dead leaves scattered over the black asphalt; red, the leaves still clinging to the trees against a background of blue sky. The sunlight, gentle and luminous, shone upon the leaves. Then all of a sudden I felt happy. Yes indeed, happy! Happy because I was beautiful, because I was young, because I was overflung with health, because I was the wife of a well-known and highly esteemed architect. So happy that, as I drove my car from one avenue to the next, outside the town, suddenly I started to sing.

But all at once I fell silent and my heart sank. On a notice-board at the opening of a country lane I read 'Villa Mimosa. Nursing Home'.

More dead than alive, I parked the car in the open space in front of the clinic, which looked like any ordinary modern hotel, with its projecting porch, its glass doors, its lines of windows on two floors. But it was precisely this hypocritical look which frightened me. I should have preferred a real mental hospital, with bars at the windows, white-clothed orderlies, the air of a prison. I went into the entrance hall, in every way similar to the normal hall of an hotel. But in the corners, in armchairs or on sofas, sat groups of people *who did not speak to each other*. Why did they not speak to each other? I went over to the porter's desk and enquired in a faint voice for Tania. After a brief telephone conversation I was told that my friend was expecting me in Room No. 14 on the first floor. I made my way to the lift.

The place *has an effect* upon one, there is no doubt about it, it *has an effect*. As soon as the lift started to rise, I went close to the mirror and put out my tongue, a horrible tongue, big, red and pointed, which I did not know I possessed, and I made a face at myself. Then asked aloud, 'Who are you?'

The lift stopped, the doors opened, I stepped out and went along the corridor.

I came to door No. 14. I knocked, and Tania's voice bade me come in. I entered the room. Teak furniture, in the Swedish style; the shutters were closed, the lamp on the bedside table was alight. Tania was lying on the bed, crosswise. But as soon as I came in she jumped to her feet and hurried to push the table against the door. My heart started beating faster. 'Why d'you bar the door?' I asked.

'Because there's no key. D'you understand? There's no key.'

I watched her as she turned and threw herself back on the bed. She was dark, tall, supple, with a full, rounded figure. And with a doll-like, affected face, a too-perfect oval, eyes that were too sweet, a mouth that was too pretty. I did not find her very much changed, apart from her pallor and a curious look which was at the same time both faded and mischievous. I felt agitated, and, as I sat down on the bed, I said, 'You don't say so! There's no key? Is that really so?'

'Yes, that's how it is. Anybody can come in.'

'And ... do they come in?'

She shrugged her shoulders. 'Yes, they come in, under various pretexts. But don't make me say what I don't want to say.'

'Pretexts? So they come in for ... other reasons.'

'Of course. All of them: doctors, orderlies, waiters.'

'And you?'

'I defend myself as best I can. Last night I threw the telephone at the head of a waiter who wanted to come in with the excuse of a bottle of mineral water which I hadn't ordered.'

She rolled her eyes in a strange manner and I followed this rolling of her eyes with growing anxiety. In a low voice I asked, 'But now tell me: why did you do it?'

'Do what?'

'Why did you take the barbiturates?'

'Ugh! Because I didn't want to go on living in a world like this.'

I could only approve of what she said. Hurriedly, feverish-

ly, I said, 'Quite right. How can one possibly live in a world
like this?'

'That's what I wonder, too.'

Suddenly there was a knock at the door. Tania grew pale.
'There they are,' she murmured. 'Now we're in for it.'

'Who are "they"?'

'The doctor's visit.'

From outside the door, a loud male voice demanded, 'Can
I come in?'

Tania replied at once, energetically, 'Of course you can't.'

The voice, soft but authoritative, insisted, 'Of course it's
"you can't come in" for just anybody, but for me it's "you
can".' And at the same time the door-handle was turned
and someone pushed against the door. Tania leapt to her
feet, went and placed herself against the table, trying to prop
it up with her own body. But the person who was pushing it
was stronger than she. Gradually the door opened slightly.
And then, through the opening, the doctor and the nurse
slipped into the room.

The doctor looked like a sportsman. Thickset, he had a
brown, vigorous-looking face, hair cut *en brosse*, dark brown
eyes, a short nose, a black moustache. He was wearing a
white coat; but I could well imagine him in a velvet jacket,
corduroy trousers, Wellington boots, with a dog beside him
and a double-barrelled gun slung over his shoulder. The
nurse was fair-haired and bony, with a triangular face. As
she saw them come in, Tania made a gesture of despair and
ran and threw herself on the bed again. The doctor held out
his strong, stocky, hairy hand to her, saying, 'Come on,
come on, don't be angry with me. Let's shake hands, like
good friends.'

Tania, subdued and at the same time fearful, very slowly
lifted her hand; gallantly, the doctor kissed it. I could not
help thinking, for some reason, that, in Tania's place, it
would have been *I* who kissed the doctor's hand. I introduced myself in an agitated voice: 'My name's Eleonora.
I'm a friend of Tania's. How is Tania, doctor?'

'She's getting on well. We shall soon be sending her home.

If she takes her pill now, we shall send her home a day earlier.'

As he said this, he made a sign to the nurse who promptly stepped forward holding a glass of water in one hand and, in the other, a big white tablet. Tania said, with decision, 'I'm not taking any pills.'

'Come along, come along.'

'No, when I say no, I mean no.'

'Come along, come along.'

The doctor made a sign to the nurse, then put out his hand and, with just two fingers, grasped Tania's face at the joints of the jaw-bones. I saw Tania, subdued, perhaps, rather than forced, open her mouth, making a curious grimace; the doctor immediately inserted the pill into it and then poured into it a little water. Tania swallowed, and I could see the convulsive movements of her throat as she gulped it down. The doctor relaxed his grip. Tania threw herself down on the bed with her face in the pillow. The doctor stroked her head in a fatherly, affectionate way. Then he said to me, 'Your friend's all right. Home soon!'

The moment the door was closed, I flung myself upon Tania. With some anxiety I said to her, 'Here's an idea. The doctor says you're all right. Then why should you stay here? Here are the keys of my car. You must pretend to be a visitor, leave the house, get into the car and drive first of all to see my husband. Tell him that I felt ill, that I've asked the doctor to take me in, that I've already taken a room, and that he must come and see me in, let us say, four or five days. As for you yourself, leave the car with my husband and go back quietly to your own home.'

If you could have seen Tania! She got up at once from the bed and said, 'Right, that's agreed. But I must pack my bag.'

'Never mind your bag. I'll see you get your things to-morrow. Easy, because I'll stay in your room. You go away and I take your place.'

She said nothing. Agitated but cheerful, she remarked, 'Well, I'll go and tidy myself a little and then I'll be ready.' So saying, she disappeared by another door into the bath-room.

Everything had gone so rapidly that I had had no time to reflect. But as soon as Tania had disappeared, the first impulse was succeeded by a slight reaction of reasonable prudence. Very well, I would take Tania's place; that evening the doctor would come, would make me open my mouth with his powerful fingers and force me to swallow the pill; into that room in which it was impossible to lock the door there would come, under various pretexts, that night, orderlies and waiters; this was all very well, but what would happen between Tania and my husband? Tania was unmarried, she lived alone, she was good-looking, she was known for her sentimental unscrupulousness, to put it mildly; she might get it into her head to make a kind of exchange: 'You take my place at the clinic, I'll take yours at your home.' Mind what you're doing!

I did not have one single moment's hesitation. I heard Tania singing to herself in the bathroom, putting the last touches to her *toilette*, no doubt with the idea, already, of making herself beautiful and seductive for the moment when she would present herself to my husband. I jumped down off the bed and tiptoed out of the room. Two minutes later I was at the wheel of my car and already out of the nursing-home car park.

And there again were the red leaves on the trees, the yellow leaves on the asphalt, the soft, luminous sunlight on the leaves, the sky blue and radiant behind the leaves. Suddenly I felt happy. Yes indeed, happy! Happy because I was beautiful, because I was young, because I was overflowing with health, because I was the wife of a well-known and highly esteemed architect who at the moment was waiting for me at home.

TWO LAPSES

My husband and I hide nothing from one another. Every evening at dinner we tell one another what we have done during the day. We do not do this deliberately, programmatically. Since we love one another and have no secrets from one another, we do it naturally, almost without being aware of it. Not so much, perhaps, in order to acquire information as to nullify, by means of our statements, the daily separation caused by differences of occupation. I introduce my husband, so to speak, into the life that I have lived without him and he does the same with me. Once these statements of ours have come to an end, our two lives, like twin rivers which have been flowing for a while separated and are then reunited, become once again one single life.

Today, as usual, we were sitting at table. It was hot; the french-window on to the garden was wide open; in the night the darkness of the flower-beds could be seen starred with pale flowers which had come out during these days in May. My husband looked at the flowers, looked at me and then said, 'You're like those flowers.'

'What d'you mean?'

'You also come into bloom with the spring. You are really "flowering", as they say. Or "florid". Or again *en fleur*, like Proust's *jeunes filles*. You have colour in your cheeks, brightness in your eyes, glossy hair, shining teeth. Really one would like to know what you have done to become so beautiful, to have such a look of happiness.'

'My love, I haven't done anything, I've led my usual life—that is, nothing new, nothing extraordinary. Just the usual routine, neither more nor less. First of all I went to see Dirce who has opened her new boutique, a most successful affair, nothing but plastic and plexiglass and steel. As soon as I went in, I went to Dirce and told her I felt very unhappy because this year spring had caught me by surprise, so to speak, and I had nothing but the things from last year and was almost ashamed to leave the house. D'you know what Dirce did? She told me to shut my eyes, led me to a door, pushed me into a room and then told me to open my eyes again. I did so, and then, out of gratitude, I threw my arms round her neck and embraced her. Just imagine! On a big table there were all sorts of shorts, of hotpants, of short trousers, of loose trousers. And besides, all round, on coat-hangers, an infinity of ready-to-wear clothes of every shape and design. Truly, I almost felt my head going round and I told Dirce to leave me alone and so I stayed in that big room for two hours and by the end of two hours I had reorganized the whole of my wardrobe. Having thus solved the problem of the spring, and feeling much lighter and happier, I paid a visit that I had put off I don't know how many times; I went to see Giorgina who had a baby a month ago. I found her in the midst of nappies and feeding bottles; we chatted about this and that and then I left her because she had to feed the baby, and seeing it was seven o'clock and I had at least an hour to wander round it occurred to me to pop in at a certain gallery in Via del Babuino; so I went there and found there was a very interesting show of pictures by a painter I know by sight—but I can't remember his name, you must help me—a tall, dark chap with hair all over the place and long side-whiskers and a sort of haunted look in his eyes. Well, I looked at the pictures one by one and then, suddenly, the painter arrived and we talked and, what with one thing and another, he told me he would like to give me a drawing and why didn't I come and choose one for myself at his studio which was just round the corner in Via Margutta, and I said yes, partly because it was still early and I didn't want to come back home. So we went to the studio in Via Margutta, up little staircases and through little court-yards, and, once we were in the studio, he showed me a big portfolio full of drawings and then, what with this and that, we made love and, after we had made love, he wrote on the drawing I had chosen a really charming dedication for me: "To Diana, the most beautiful, my most beautiful drawing"; then he went back with me to the gallery. All of a sudden I remembered that there was a cocktail party at

Lorenza's, at the Janiculum, and it so happened that the painter (I can't really recall his name, but it's written below the drawing) was going there too and so, quite naturally, I told him I would drive him there in my car. We went to the Janiculum—what an effort!—there was an unbelievable amount of traffic and I took a whole hour, and then when we arrived we found an enormous crowd there and I lost my painter. What was I to do? I hunted for him for some time and then gave up, thinking that he could always find some-one or other to give him a lift back. So, not knowing what to do, I started chatting with Pietro—Pietro, you know?—but waiters were going past with trays, first I took one glass, then a second, then a third, and in the end, you won't be-lieve it, I was drunk and really I don't know how I managed to drive back here. But wait, I want to show you the drawing, I want you to tell me if you like it. Wait.'

Excitedly I rose from the table, ran into the bedroom and there was the rolled-up drawing on the bed, together with my handbag and the car-keys. I took up the drawing, started taking off the elastic band that held it together and then, all of a sudden, I stopped, petrified, my eyes staring, as I realized that, carried away by our intimacy, by euphoria and perhaps also by the drunkenness from those three or four glasses I had drunk at Lorenza's, I had told my hus-band to his face that I had been unfaithful to him.

I suddenly recollected that, in the country one day, in a farmyard, I had watched a sow which, snout to the ground, had gone round devouring everything that she came across. Ceaselessly poking round, she had eaten a cabbage-stalk, then an apple, then a live newly-hatched chick which, before it disappeared into her mouth, had just had time to utter a desperate cheeping; then another apple, another cabbage-stalk, a piece of water-melon peel, another apple . . .

I myself had behaved like that sow. I had mentioned one unimportant thing, then another, then I had said that I had made love with the painter and had then added a lot of other unimportant things, all this without making any dis-tinctions, levelling everything down, indeed, in the euphoria of indiscriminate, inebriated intimacy. These reflections, for some reason, restored my courage. I shook my head, took up the drawing and returned to the dining-room.

My husband, during by absence, had lit a cigarette and was now sitting still, smoking, with eyes downcast. It was not possible to understand exactly what he was thinking. Without sitting down, I unfolded the rolled-up drawing and showed it to him. 'What d'you think of it?'

'It's not bad.'

I sat down again. The maid came in with the tray and we helped ourselves. Then, in a perfectly natural way, I asked him, 'And you, what have you done today?'

As though he had been merely waiting for this question, he answered me at once, 'I've had a pretty interesting day, too, perfectly normal. I went to the office and I've been working all day. Then in the evening, everyone went away, but I stayed on, and as my secretary, Flora, also stayed on, we took advantage of it to make love. Then I finished off a few little things, and just as I was leaving, guess who telephoned? Tommaso. He asked me what we were doing this evening and I told him we might meet and possibly even go together to the cinema. Did I do wrong?'

Stupidly, appalled, I stammered, 'You did extremely wrong.'

'In what way? In making an appointment with Tommaso? Never mind, I'll telephone him now and tell him we can't manage it.'

'No, no, in being unfaithful to me with that terribly vulgar secretary of yours.'

We looked one another in the face for a moment; then he broke out into a loud, frank burst of laughter. 'Now be honest,' he said. 'You believed what I said.'

'Believed what?'

'That I was unfaithful to you with Flora. But it's not true. Flora left with the others. And I should never dream of making love with her. Don't worry, I haven't been unfaithful.'

'But *I* have.' The words slipped out unintentionally.

'When? Where? How? With whom?'

He fired off all these questions at me point-blank, looking

fixedly at me, with insistence. I remained silent for a little, trying to collect my ideas. Then he came to my assistance: 'You gave me a full account of your day and in that account you never mentioned betrayals. That means that you have been unfaithful to me before today. But then, be precise: when? where? how? with whom?'

Suddenly I understood. These questions he was asking, this look he gave me implied, 'Come on, cheer up! You were unfaithful in an absent-minded way and you mentioned it in an absent-minded way. I prefer to think that nothing happened and I, in my turn, will pretend to be absent-minded and not to have heard or understood anything. But if you insist on telling me you've been unfaithful, then it's no longer a mere lapse, it's then a serious thing. So accept my absent-mindedness just as I've accepted yours. Is that agreed?'

Almost without meaning to, I nodded. 'I'm sorry,' I said, 'I spoke without really meaning it. Perhaps it was from a sudden feeling of guilt which...'

'Which made you imagine you had done something which in reality you hadn't done.'

USEFUL

We got out of the car and walked along the road. On one side there was a hedge of elder-bushes, with thick, dark foliage. On the other, an immense field of wheat, still green and lustrous, stretched right to the horizon which was blocked, over its whole length, by the limestone barrier of the tall buildings of Rome. As if to recapitulate our discussion, I said to him, 'I can't devote myself entirely to you. My work absorbs me. I'm never sure of being free, not even on Sundays. We can see one another now and again, that's all.'

'Yes, once every two months.'

For a moment I felt bewildered. Two months? Was it already two months? 'No, not two months,' I said. 'At the most it must be a month and a half.'

'Two months and one day. We met last time on 27th March. Today's 29th May.'

'All right, then: two months. I've been busy.'

'But may I know what it is you've been doing?'

Again I had a moment of bewilderment. I recovered myself at once and replied, 'What I do concerns only myself. I've been working.'

'But do you love me or don't you?'

A third moment of bewilderment. Did I love him? I looked inside myself, as one looks inside a cupboard to see if a certain object is there; and I found nothing. Then I looked at him and realized that I liked him. He had an awkward but vigorous-looking head, with thick, bright hair growing halfway down his forehead, shining eyes, a hooked nose and a rather brutal mouth. Yes, I liked him; but it was precisely this fact of my liking him that aroused in me a sense of insufficiency and discontent. I answered in a faint voice, 'Yes, certainly I love you, you know that.'

'Then why don't we see each other more?'

Feeling bewildered again, for the fourth time, I replied, 'I don't know. Perhaps because love is such an egotistical feeling. It isolates the two of us; one thinks only about love and everything else is unimportant. And so suddenly one feels horribly egotistical and useless. Above all, useless. The feeling of being useful to other people, to everybody, which work gives me—love never gives me that feeling. And so, in a way, I never find time to devote myself to love. It seems to me—how shall I put it?—a waste of time.'

'Work? But what work?'

'What work? Why, work.'

The hedge beside which we were walking had at this point a narrow opening. Two or three dusty, stony steps dug out of the slope provided a passage from the level of the road to that of the field stretching away behind the hedge. 'Let's go up there,' he suggested. 'We can lie on the grass.'

I agreed. With one bound he was at the top of the gap, then he held out his hand to me and I climbed up too. In the field the grass was long and thick after that rainy month of May. And down on the far side was the tree beneath which, no doubt, we should lie. Then, when my trousers became caught in a thorny branch, I looked down. And there thrust deep into the tangle of the hedge, I caught sight of a number of objects: a half-used roll of toilet-paper; a piece of pink soap; a large comb made of bone, a woman's comb, greasy and blackened; a white wooden brush, moulting and full of hairs; and an empty, worn-out handbag. It seemed to me that these objects soiled not only the hedge but the whole countryside. Filled with repugnance, I asked, 'Look! What's all this stuff?'

Calmly he replied, 'I should imagine it's the toilet apparatus of a rustic type of street-walker, one of those that lurk on country roads.'

Then he started off along a vague, narrow path which wound through the long grass and looked as if it might have been trodden by the feet of the owner of those same objects and those of her men. 'No,' I exclaimed, 'I'm not going to that tree over there. It's there that the owner of those disgusting objects works, so to speak. I can't lie down in the place where *she* lies down.'

He did not answer me but continued to walk in the direction of the tree. I called to him to stop; he shrugged his shoulders. I ran after him to hold him back; he turned, seized me by the wrist, tried to pull me towards a bed of crushed, downtrodden grass under the tree, which had without doubt been produced by the bodies of the prostitute and her clients. I was overcome by a feeling of frantic repugnance, I struggled with him as he sought sadistically to throw me down on that natural and much-used bed. Finally I managed to free myself and run away. He did not follow me, but remained under the tree calling after me in a vicious way, 'What airs you put on! Who d'you think you are? That woman who works here is better than you. She at least makes herself useful.'

Feeling overwrought and angry, but conscious that within a week we should have made peace again, I ran to the car and drove straight home to the Parioli district. I rushed into my flat, a little top-floor flat in a smart block; I undressed, put on a dressing-gown and sat down at my typewriter in front of the window. The position of my body as I sat with my legs close together and my bust erect, the quiet light of the sky through the window, the sight of my hands on the keys of the typewriter—all these at once instilled in me a special kind of tranquillity, at the same time both cynical and deluded. I knew perfectly well that the article I was preparing to write, a report on a festival of light music, was a thing of no value in which, furthermore, I should not be expressing myself in any way; but at the same time the writing of this article gave me the feeling that I was making myself useful, and effectively so. I am not a cultivated person, I have read scarcely anything, I have remained the ignoramus that I was when I finished secondary school; nevertheless I had for some time been writing articles and short stories which I then succeeded, with more or less difficulty, in having accepted by the so-called 'women's magazines'. In actual fact the act of writing gives me more pleasure than voicing something that I feel or think. It gives me pleasure because, as I have said, it produces a sense of tranquillity and makes me feel useful. Today too, in fact, after I had been at the typewriter for four hours on end, when I had finished and re-assembled the pages of the article and tidied up my desk and placed the cover over the machine, I was conscious of a feeling of hilarity and comfort as of a duty accomplished.

I rose from the table, went into the bathroom to take a shower, dressed myself with great care, put the article into my bag and hurried out of the house. The porter, greeting me from his box, made me feel an acute pride in my usefulness: he was not greeting one of the many society dolls who inhabit the building; he was greeting someone who feels and *is* useful. In a short time I was in the midst of the Roman traffic. From high up on a lorry, a couple of ill-mannered drivers, at the sight of my splendid legs with my feet alternating on the pedals, threw me tiresome compliments. What did it matter? I did not see them and I did not hear them. Yet another effect of usefulness.

I parked my car, went to an old building behind the Piazzale Flaminio, climbed four flights of stairs, pushed open a door and went in. This was the office of the magazine for which I had written the article. In the corridor the doors were open, and inside the rooms one could see shorthand typists seated at their tables and sub-editors in shirt-sleeves behind their desks. I reached the editor's door and opened it without knocking. The editor himself was reading a manuscript and made a sign to me to sit down. He was a man of about forty, with a surly, sleepy look and a round face, plump and with minute features. I sat and waited, with the article in my hand. At last he looked up. 'Did you write it? Give it here.'

I handed him the article; he started reading it and I looked round the room. Suddenly I felt as though I had been anaesthetized. It was the second time I had been in that room; but, for some reason, it was as if it were the first time because I did not remember very clearly what had happened a week earlier, when I had introduced myself in order to suggest myself as a contributor. Or rather, I remembered it but it was as though it had happened in a dream, the dream that constitutes my life when I do not feel myself to be useful; and has anyone ever believed that a dream is reality? The editor's voice made me start. 'Look,' he said; 'this won't do.'

'But I ...'

'I wanted to try you out and sent you to this festival of light music in the hope that you would write something that was free and easy, ironical, witty. Instead of which you bring me a school essay. And with several grammatical mistakes, into the bargain.'

'Those could be corrected.'

'It's not a question of correcting, it's a question of re-writing.'

I did not know what to say, I felt bewildered. He was staring at me now with a kind of obstinate, angry curiosity. Finally he asked, 'D'you have to write in order to live?'

'Not really. I could live on what my father allows me.'

'Then why don't you give up writing, seeing that you're not cut out for it?'

I said nothing; I felt more and more bewildered; my eyes roamed all round the room and finally came to a stop at an old and discoloured green divan which took up the whole of the far wall. It was an object that was familiar to me; either I had seen it before or it resembled something I had already seen. I bit my lips, hesitated, then made up my mind; I rose from my chair, walked round the desk, stooped down towards the editor and, skimming his plump, well-shaven cheek with my lips, sought his mouth with my own. He kissed me, then took up my manuscript again, re-read it or at least pretended to re-read it, too excited by now to know what he was doing; and, when I asked him, 'Then you don't think it could be corrected?' he nodded his head. Then he sighed, put the manuscript on his desk, placed a paper-weight on top of it, put his arm round my waist and rose with an effort from his armchair. Thus entwined, we made our way together towards the green divan. I had time to notice a big stain, like a coffee-stain, on one of the cushions. Then I lay down underneath him.

Afterwards I went away. The editor had returned to his place behind the desk and gave me a very slight bow. From the door I cast a glance at the green divan and again had the strange feeling that it was something I had seen before, or rather, that it was something that had already come into my life. I went out.

Once I was in the street, I realized I had nothing to do and that nevertheless I did not wish to return home. For once the tranquillizing image of the typewriter on my table in front of the window for some reason disgusted me. There was still daylight, and almost without knowing what I was doing I drove along the Via Flaminia until I was outside Rome. I reached the road where, in the early afternoon, I had stopped with my lover, and there was the hedge. I stopped the car, got out and started walking, until I came to the gap in the hedge. After a moment's hesitation, I clambered right up through the gap into the field. In the fading twilight I could again see the path through the thick, tall grass, and then, in the distance, the tree. But the toilet articles had vanished; the prostitute, having finished her work, had collected them and gone away. I walked forward and came to the space under the tree and the bed of crushed, downtrodden grass formed by the bodies of the prostitute and her clients. Once more, I had the strange impression of something seen before, or rather, of something that had been part of my life, just as shortly before when I had looked at the green divan in the editor's room. Actually the divan had recalled the grassy bed, as now the bed recalled the divan. Suddenly I had a cruel desire to humiliate, to punish myself. Overcoming my repugnance, I lay down in the space of trampled grass which, in fact, exactly fitted my own body. I lay on my back, I closed my eyes, pressing my lids against my cheeks, trying to force a tear. I did not succeed.

MOTHER LOVE

Our two children oppose us with such incredible and pitiless violence that my husband and I, caught off-balance in the middle years of our lives (we are both of us less than forty), do not know what to do. Two or three years ago, when news reached us from all sides of the revolt of children against their parents, we were still able to deceive ourselves into thinking that our own children would constitute an exception. Patrizia and Corrado, without being particularly affectionate, behaved in a normal manner, just as, fundamentally, we have behaved with our own parents. Then, suddenly, on their return from a holiday spent in a seaside camp with people of their own age, they burst forth against us with a fury which seemed to derive its force from the delay with which it showed itself. Certainly it could not be said that they had not made up for lost time! Normal children, indeed! Respect and affection, far from it! Patrizia and Corrado became so enraged with us that we ought to have considered them as a couple of enemies and treated them accordingly, that is, to have broken off all relations with them. Alas, however, it was not so. They were our children and their hatred was derived, simply and solely, from the fact that they were our children. So that we, in our turn, were forced to recognize in that hatred the surest sign of the bond of blood that united us.

I have said that we were caught off-balance and I must explain what I mean. My husband and I were both of us in that middle age in which people attain their definitive form and when what has been, has been: they are not going to change any more. In opposing us in this savage manner, our children were, in reality, taunting us for the form we had taken, to attain which we had taken pains for so many years. It was, so to speak, as though they were taunting a caterpillar for turning into a butterfly, a flower for having come into bloom. What was worse, their hatred made us suspect that we had been transformed into very ugly butterflies, into stinking flowers. Hatred, in fact, is a kind of mirror in which the hated person cannot help seeing himself reflected with a repugnant image.

Naturally Patrizia and Corrado hate us each in his or her own way, according to their own characters. Patrizia, a good-looking girl actually too fully-formed and striking, shows her hatred in an emotional, impetuous way. During squabbles at table (we meet only at mealtimes, the rest of the time we lead separate lives) Patrizia, after barely two or three encounters in the customary verbal duel, loses her temper, works herself into a fury, shouts, bursts into tears and leaves the room, banging the door behind her. Corrado, on the other hand, is calm and controlled; he gives an impression of calculation and premeditation with the stammerings that slow down his speech and make one think that he is carefully choosing the most vicious and offensive words. With Corrado it is very often I myself who give up the struggle and rise from the table, indignant and with my eyes filled with tears.

One day I decided to make a final attempt at reconciliation. It was early afternoon; I was lying on the bed in the dark beside my husband who was asleep; at lunch there had been an even more bitter encounter than usual, and I was still feeling seriously upset. Suddenly seized with unexpected impatience, I got off the bed and started dressing in a hurry, in the half-darkness. I decided to go first to Patrizia, who was resting in her room; then I would seek out Corrado in his study. I would be rational and judicious; just and well-balanced; understanding and lucid. I would indeed be capable of managing the affair with the superiority that I derived from experience and affection. Thinking it over, I was reassured and felt calmer. But then, inexplicably, and in an almost automatic way, I did a disconcerting thing: slowly and cautiously I opened a locker, took out my husband's flat, heavy revolver and slipped it into the big pocket of my safari jacket.

Well then, I would make an attempt. I left the room on tiptoe without making any noise, went to the far end of the corridor and opened Patrizia's door. For a moment I was dazzled. The two windows were wide open, the sun was pouring in. Patrizia, naked, was lying on the bed, her feet in the air and her head down, her hair dangling. She was reading a book which she held at a great distance from her eyes. From the radio on the floor came muffled music.

At my appearance Patrizia quickly pulled herself up, as though caught in a guilty act. She sat with her legs crossed, pushing back her hair, hiding her breasts with her arms across them. I too sat down on the bed, at no great distance from her. I had thought I would get to the root of the question at once; but for a moment all I could do was to look at her in silence. Her face was heavy and childish, her hair of exceptional thickness; her body was splendid, of a luminous whiteness, a powerful, indolent solidity. There on the opposite wall a large looking-glass showed the two of us: beside the naked Patrizia, so exuberant and full of vitality, I myself looked dried-up and at the same time faded, in my tight jacket, and with the drawn, carefully made-up features of my face. What was the relationship between myself and Patrizia? For the first time I recalled that I was her mother, not in an affectionate but in a physical sense: her opulence had issued from my dryness, her exuberance from my decay. In a voice that I knew was harsh and disagreeable, I said, 'Patrizia, I've come to talk to you.'

She answered without turning, already hostile, and she too was looking at the mirror opposite. 'To talk to me? What an honour!'

'Patrizia, we can't go on like this.'

'Quite true, but don't worry. As quickly as possible, as soon as I've found a job, I'll relieve you of my presence.'

'But we don't in the least want you to go away. We're fond of you and we want you to stay with us. But in the meantime we should like you at any rate to explain why it is you're so angry with us.'

She shrugged her shoulders and was silent. Again I looked at her, first directly and then in the glass. I had a jealous, anxious feeling which is difficult to describe: as though I found myself confronted with an object which was not only my property but of my own creation, but which, somehow or other, had made itself independent of me. I could not help adding, 'But don't you realize that you can't treat your mother like this, your mother who brought you into the world, who suckled you and brought you up?'

'Please, for goodness sake! I felt sure physiology was going to be dragged in! For goodness sake!'

'Anyhow, you owe us an explanation.'

'But of what?'

'Of your absurd hostility.'

She did not reply. She shrugged her shoulders. I moved close to her (and all the time I could not help watching the scene in the looking-glass), I put my arm round her shoulders and said to her, 'Trizia, what have you got against us?'

She took hold of my hand, removed my arm from her shoulders as one might remove a scarf that is too warm. 'Hands off!' she said. 'And anyhow there's nothing to explain. Wer'e angry with you both because you are what you are.'

'Well, what are we?'

I awaited her reply anxiously. My hand went into the pocket of my jacket and I grasped the butt of the pistol. All of a sudden, as often happened with her, Patrizia flew into a rage. 'What are you?' she said. 'It's just that you're disgusting. And don't ask me why you're disgusting. You're disgusting because you're disgusting: and that's all there is to it. And now be kind enough to go away; I want to be alone and above all I don't want to see you.' She rose, seized me by the arm and tried to drag me towards the door. For a moment we struggled, she naked and I clothed, she enveloped in light, I in shadow. In the meantime I was gripping the pistol at the bottom of my pocket and telling myself that very soon I should pull my hand out. Then an unexpected thing happened. Patrizia stopped in the doorway, let go of me and said, 'I'm sorry, you make me lose my head. Please go away. It will be better for both of us.' Out of breath, I looked at her in silence, saying to myself that I had been on the point of planting real bullets of steel in that luminous flesh of hers which was, in fact, my very own flesh. I went out.

I went straight to Corrado's study, threw open the door violently and stood there in astonishment: the room was empty. And yet he had said at lunch that day he was expecting a friend so that they could do their work together. I closed the door, went over to the table and looked at the typewriter, the books, the papers. My son was not merely studying at the university; he was also reading and writing on his own. The desk was covered with books; there was one book lying open on the sofa; two shelves were laden with books lined up in a double row, in an order which to me was mysterious. I sat down on the sofa and haphazardly picked up the open book, my son's most recent reading. I tried to read it but could not succeed in doing so. It was written in Italian certainly: but the sense of the phrases evaded me. It was written in a different language from that of the books I usually read. This language was not so much obscure as evasive, foreign, elusive. In the turn of the sentences, in the choice of terms, in the general meaning I recognized the same cold, premeditated hostility that Corrado displayed in his relations with his father and myself.

Or perhaps it was not so much a question of hostility as of expulsion and rejection. This book repudiated my understanding, my sympathy, my curiosity. It was like Corrado, like Patrizia: it shut itself up, it excluded me. The general sense of what I was trying in vain to read appeared to me like a high wall, smooth and entirely without openings.

In any case I was too disturbed to read. My heart was still beating very fast after my encounter with Patrizia. The words echoed in my dismayed incomprehension like sounds that were precise and clear but without meaning. This, indeed, was a foreign language for people who to me were foreign. A language, in fact, for the initiated. I did not belong among those who understood it; Corrado and Patrizia did. All of a sudden I felt overwhelmed by the same obscure jealousy that I had experienced in the face of my daughter's nudity. Once again the absurd thought crossed my mind, 'All this came out of me. And now it is rebelling against me.'

The book slipped from my hand and fell on the floor; and almost automatically I placed my foot upon it. Then I moved my foot in such a way that the heel of my shoe should tear the pages. Then I twisted my heel strongly, and the page, in fact two or three pages, were torn out. In the meantime, however, I was looking at the door, fearing that my son might come in unexpectedly and find me busy destroying, like a madwoman, the book that he was in the course of reading.

I should have liked to spit on the book, to soil it, to turn it into a piece of refuse to be thrown into the dustbin. I recalled seeing once, in an old house in the country, a book hanging up in the lavatory, for a purpose which can be imagined. I should have liked the book I was trampling on to finish up in the same way. What was happening to me?

In the end I did nothing. I got up, leaving the book on the floor, and went out. I went back, on tiptoe, to my bedroom, took off my shoes and lay down in the dark beside my husband.

Something was causing me discomfort, under my hip. It was the gun. I pulled it out of my pocket and for a moment weighed it in my hand. I pointed it, for a joke, against my temple. I reflected that my children, fundamentally, would like me to kill myself. But they were deluding themselves: I was not going to kill myself. I was a mother who loved her children whatever they did; a mother who was capable of finding an unshakable superiority in her great love. I was a mother to whom, in the end, children would inevitably return after being defeated by that very same world into which, willy-nilly, she had introduced them.

NAZI

Many are the ups and downs of life! Having started as a teacher of literature, I have now landed, owing to my uncommon beauty, in the unexpected profession of actress in photo-romances, those stories told by means of photographs and captions. At this moment, for instance, I am acting the part of a wicked heroine of the Nazi type. I wear hotpants, a leather jerkin, jackboots of black leather; round my arm is a red band upon which the black swastika stands out against a white background. Other swastikas adorn my peaked cap, the lapels of my jacket, the buckle of my belt. I kill my victims with a pistol, I torture them with a whip, with a knife, with my spurs. Naturally my exuberant bosom bursts forth out of my jacket which, for some reason or other, is always half-open. My hotpants are so short that they expose my legs right up to my groin and so low in the waist that they leave my stomach bare. I am wicked, in short, but beautiful. Herein lies the secret of my success with the numerous lovers of the photo-romance. If I was beautiful and good, or ugly and wicked, I should not have any attraction. The truth of the matter is that I appear beautiful because I am wicked and appear wicked because I am beautiful.

In real life, on the other hand, apart from being dark-haired (I wear a wig, since Nazis *have* to be blonde), I am a reasonable, reserved, controlled character. I am polite to everyone but I keep my distance. And I have a horror of violence. The mere idea of striking an adversary fills me with disgust. In my opinion, words should suffice. That evening I had just come back from work. Usually I take off my make-up and change my clothes at the studios. But I wanted to be quick, I jumped into my car in my Nazi costume and came straight home. Exhausted by the usual orgy of cruelty in the photo-romance, I lay back in an armchair, my cap pulled down on top of my wig, my whip across my

knees. I was smoking, and was surprised when my servant
Michelina appeared in the doorway.

She is a small woman, very robust and with a head like
a statue. Not a beautiful statue, however. An ugly statue of
a housewife or a matron, of the kind that can be seen carved
on Etruscan sarcophagi. A low, narrow forehead, eyes like
those of a hen, a beaky nose and a sullen mouth. Michelina,
before she came to me, had been in the house of a so-called
'signora' for fifteen years. I, on the other hand, was known
to her as the 'signorina'. The 'signora' had died, otherwise
Michelina would still be with her.

With many hesitations and roundabout remarks Michelina told me, in conclusion, that she wished to leave me. I
was amazed. I had thought, in all good faith, that I was an
exemplary mistress. Was it perhaps that I did not treat
Michelina as an equal, but as a stranger who happened to be
living under the same roof and yet doing a job that was
different from mine? In any case Michelina, for me, *was* a
stranger. How could she not have been?

Finally I said, 'But, Michelina, why is it you want to
leave? Are you not happy here?'

'No, it's not that.'

'Don't I pay you enough?'

'It's not that.'

'Is there too much work, then?'

'No, not that.'

'Don't you get enough free time?'

'Signorina, what should I do with free time?'

'What is it, then?'

'I feel too lonely.'

To tell the truth, I had never thought of this. Looking at
Michelina, I was silent. Her head was truly Etruscan, even
to the yellow terracotta colour. But she was a weeping
Etruscan, a strange, disconcerting sight. 'Why don't you
make any friends?' I asked. 'For example, the porter's
family . . .'

She shrugged her shoulders. I persevered, 'There are other
maids in the building, it's possible that . . .'

A second shrug of the shoulders. I resumed, 'Your sister, your brother ...'

A third shrug. Michelina sniffed, wiped her eyes with the back of her hand and finally said, 'For you, Signorina, I don't exist. That's why I feel lonely.'

Slightly annoyed, I replied, 'I'm a working woman. If I wasn't a photo-romance actress, I should be teaching; and you wouldn't see any more of me.'

She said nothing. I asked haphazardly, 'In the place where you were before you came to me, did you feel lonely there too?'

She protested sharply. 'Lonely? My goodness! The signora was on top of me all day long. She was a real torment.'

Logically, I remarked: 'Michelina, you contradict yourself. You don't like it here because you're lonely. You didn't like it there because you were never lonely. You must make up your mind.'

'The signora was on top of me, that's true,' she said, 'but she was fond of me. And I was fond of her. You're not fond of me.'

Michelina was lying. The signora was not fond of her, she made her work like a slave, she had an atrocious character. Michelina, on her side, was not fond of the signora, she hated her. The fact remained, however, that Michelina had stayed with the signora for fifteen years; in my case, on the other hand, after barely one year, she wanted to leave. 'So,' I said, 'you prefer the signora who tormented you, to me, who treat you well.'

'For you I don't exist.'

I thought again. I knew perfectly well what the relationship had been between Michelina and the signora. Michelina had been what mistresses call a 'treasure'. Having no fault to find with her, the signora tormented Michelina to such a degree that, in the end, the latter's nerves gave way and she 'answered back'. This was what the signora was expecting and she immediately flung herself upon Michelina, abusing her, ill-treating her and even going so far as to give her the sack. But Michelina did not leave, she never left. By that evening she had already become reconciled with the signora who, let it be noted, while reluctantly accepting the reconciliation, inflicted upon Michelina, who listened contritely, with bowed head, the further punishment of a lecture as interminable as it was humiliating. Yes indeed, the signora tormented Michelina; but it was precisely through this torment that she showed her awareness of Michelina's existence.

While I was thinking of all these things, I looked at myself in the wardrobe mirror and then, for the first time, I seemed to become conscious of the significance of my Nazi get-up. Seeing that the signora had given Michelina, by tormenting her, the impression that she existed, in theory I ought now to fling myself upon my maid and leave the marks of my whip on her large, muscular legs or actually on her terra-cotta Etruscan face. Or else throw her to the floor and trample on her with my heavy boots. Or again, cut her to bits with my hunting-knife. Ugh! But how did the Nazis, the SS, really behave? How did they manage to do it? How did they succeed, apart from anything else, in overcoming the physical impossibility of laying hands on anybody? I looked at Michelina and shuddered with disgust. I said sharply, 'Very well. Now go and bring me the shopping accounts.'

She went out and I mentally prepared myself, looking at myself in the glass as I jammed down my cap on my forehead and buttoned up my jacket. Michelina came back. She handed me the account-book. I took it with one hand while with the other I stroked my boots with the whip. I looked over the account: it was a precise certificate of Michelina's honesty and meticulousness. 'This evening,' I exclaimed, 'you've bought me a beefsteak whereas I wrote down that I wanted some fish.'

'Signora, you wrote down for me, "This evening, beef-steak", and it's beefsteak I bought.'

'No, madam: I said fish. Michelina, I didn't know that among your many faults you were also a liar.'

'I, a liar!'

'Yes, a liar.'

She rushed out impetuously and came back with a sheet of paper. 'It's beefsteak that's written here.'

'But that isn't my handwriting. You wrote that yourself. Very well, then. As well as a liar you're a forger.'

'But what d'you mean, Signorina? This is your writing.'

'I tell you you're a liar and a thief.'

'I, a thief?'

'Yes, a thief. Because with meat you can steal something, since there's not much difference between frozen and fresh meat. But with fish it's impossible to play these clever little tricks.'

'I a thief! Be careful what you say!'

'Yes, a thief; and don't raise your voice or I shall tell you that, besides being a thief, you're ill-mannered and rude and boorish.'

It was I who was now raising my voice. I stood up, flourished my whip, shouted. What an effort! What a strain! What a torment! Pursued by my long, lovely, booted legs, threatened by my whip, Michelina was terrified and rushed off into the kitchen; then, when I upset a pile of plates with a back-handed blow on to the floor, she took refuge in her own room.

Exhausted, I went back into the sitting-room. Sweat was running down my breasts, tightly enclosed as they were in my leather jerkin. I tore off my wig, I tore off my jerkin. I struggled to tear off my boots and finally succeeded. My pants, too, were thrown off. Damp, panting, I fell back into the depths of the armchair. But the Nazis, the SS, how did they manage? I should have very much liked to know how they managed. Did they perhaps eat special food? Or did they take drugs? Or again . . .

An indeterminate number of minutes followed. Not a sound came from Michelina's room. Obviously she was offended, she was frightened, she detested, hated me. But she must now be aware that she existed for me, just as she had existed for her old mistress—and more so. Ah, now she was coming.

In one hand she was carrying a suitcase, in the other a big cardboard box tied up with string. 'I'm going to my sister's,' she said. 'I'm not staying one minute longer in this house. And you'd better thank God I'm not reporting you to the police.'

The door closed and I was left alone, completely crushed. But all the time I was thinking. Michelina, then, felt that she did not exist when I treated her well. Now, however, when I had treated her badly, she had felt, just the same, that she did not exist. So what? Evidently I ought to have behaved like her old mistress. But her old mistress was dead and had carried the secret of Michelina's existence with her into the grave.

FALSE OBJECTIVES

Have you ever watched a river, trying to follow with your eyes the movements of the branch of a tree as it floated on the surface of the water? It seems as if the branch is looking for something as it goes hither and thither, pausing at inlets and then starting to move again with the current. Whereas it is not looking for anything; or rather, it is the current that causes it to move as though it is searching, and in a manner that is apparently idle and wandering but is in reality constant and tenacious. Thus, I think, has my life been hitherto. An indolent, tortuous, insidious force, the force of the vitality confined in my body as in a too-tight garment, has continually urged me on from one situation to another, from one man to another. It might be thought that —how shall I express it?—there was a method, an intention, in my restlessness. On the contrary, there was not. There was nothing except, precisely, restlessness.

What strikes me most about this force is its tortuousness. Take, for example, my marriage. I was eighteen and was the best-looking girl in the school. Extremely poor, with a widowed mother lacking in protectors or acquaintances, I became engaged to a philosophy student, Valerio, even poorer than I; and that tells everything. It seemed to me that I had made a proper choice: I loved Valerio and was loved in return; he was an intellectual and I flattered myself that I was the same. But Valerio had, as his best friend, a certain Roberto, an architect, son of a building contractor. Let me tell you now what my vitality led me into. The first thing was that it threw me into the arms of Roberto. Then it caused me to reveal to Valerio that Roberto was paying court to me, thus bringing about the rupture of their friendship. Finally it brought me into touch with Amalia, the girl who had succeeded me in Roberto's heart. Through Amalia, I went back to Roberto, brought about his reconciliation with Valerio, and organized a trip to Paris for the four of us.

But in the Simplon Tunnel, as the train was moving along in the dark, Roberto and I kissed; and then at Geneva we got out together, leaving the two betrayed ones to continue their journey. Now the best of it was that, one minute before the kiss, I still did not know that I was going to kiss Roberto. In any case, would it not have been simpler and more rational for me to go off with Roberto from the very beginning? What was the sense of this tortuousness?

We were married for five years, Roberto and I. Roberto was the correct, well-mannered, gentlemanly, but lifeless and insignificant son of an extremely rich, self-made father. His father supported us; but in exchange he insisted on his son working with him in his firm. So that I was practically alone all day long. For five years, urged on and piloted by my inscrutable vital force, I led the most social life that can be imagined. I was to be seen in all the drawing-rooms and all the resorts; I did not miss a single party, a single reception; I was always present at the places where, according to the obscure and fickle rules of snobbism, one *must* be present. Since there is no 'society' life without elegance, I was one of the best-dressed women in Rome, even though in a bizarre and conspicuous style, always rather as if I were in some ironical, comic masquerade.

In actual fact, however, in spite of all my social activity and elegance, I was searching. Even though I did not know I was searching and deceiving myself into thinking, instead, that I was occupied with social life and elegance. One afternoon, dressed almost in a Chinese style, I went to the home of some friends, to one of the usual parties. There was a great crowd there, everyone was drinking and smoking and chattering as they stood squeezed into four little narrow rooms. Then a middle-aged man, bearded and powerful, with a pipe in his mouth and dressed like a country gentleman, blockaded me in a window recess and talked to me about Indian religious thought. This man was called Tancredi; he was a landowner in the Maremma and lived in complete solitude in a villa he owned at the far end of his estate. You see how the tortuousness comes in? Instead of letting me meet Tancredi in his own neighbourhood, in

solitude, my vitality caused me to run into him in a crowd
at a party, where I should have least expected to find him.
But why?

At this point I must observe that the mysterious force
which guided me, while it was extremely slow and tortuous
in bringing me into new situations, was, on the other hand,
very expeditious in getting me out of old ones. Tancredi and
I understood one another in a trice, by the simple means of a
touching of knees which was repeated perhaps three times,
while he went on talking to me about Indian religions. Then
we left together. At the moment when I was preceding him
into the lift, he gave me a cheerful slap on the bottom, just
one. It was enough. I left a note for my husband on the dash-
board of the car; then I got into Tancredi's station-wagon.
That same evening I slept at his house in the Maremma.

So now I was living with Tancredi, in the country, on a
bare hill from which one had a view of the sea. No more
parties, no social life, no elegance. With Tancredi, life was
solitary, simple, and at the same time philosophical. We
went for walks on the beach or in the countryside; we went
shooting and riding; in the evenings, after dinner, he would
read to me aloud the texts of Indian thought and I would
listen. I was happy, or rather, I thought I was. Then, as
usual, came the abrupt, brutal contradiction of vitality.

One winter day, when Tancredi was in town doing some
shopping, I put on my coat, took the dogs with me and went
down to walk on the beach. I walked for a long time along
the glistening sand, in the grey daylight. There came towards me a young man whom I had already noticed on other
occasions: tall, pale, rather wild-eyed, with a shock of long
hair, and wearing wide trousers and a windcheater. He
greeted me and I returned his greeting; he walked beside me
and started talking and almost at once told me that he was
in love with me. I don't know what happened to me. I began
running along behind him as he, taking big steps on his long
legs, went ahead of me up over the sand-dunes towards his
little house. However we did not even get as far as the
house, so great was our impatience. A little higher up, in a
deep valley full of tin cans and scraps of plastic left there

from the summer, we rolled in one another's embrace on the cold, damp sand amongst the litter, while the dogs looked on, disconcerted, from the top of the dunes. Two days later I was in Milan, in Clelio's studio (he was a painter), once again convinced that I had sought and found.

You may wonder at the tortuous proceedings of vitality. Clelio, with whom, for a couple of weeks, I had deceived myself into thinking that I was in love, was only, so to speak, a false step. I recognized the correct step when Clelio held an exhibition in one of the best galleries. A short, stout man with a big head and black hair streaked with white followed me insistently with his eyes, wherever I went among the crowd at the exhibition. I went up to Clelio and asked him who he was. At the same moment, the man confronted us, introduced himself and then, pointing his finger at a picture, declared, 'I'll buy that.' But he said these words in so authoritative a tone and, furthermore, looking not at the picture but at me, that I had the impression that he was saying, 'I'll buy *her*'; and almost instinctively I looked at Clelio, as though to see whether he was prepared to sell me.

Erminio, for this was the buyer's name, was what is usually called by the generic term of 'financier'; and he behaved in love affairs as he did in business. That is to say, he never made a frontal assault on his adversary; on the contrary, he encircled him, by means of money. He did not buy the man, but he bought everything that surrounded and supported him. This is what he did with Clelio. Systematically he bought all his pictures, he turned him into a kind of artistic buffoon in his little court of flatterers and clients; then, when he was sure of having reduced him to a mere bundle of rags in my eyes, he ordered me to leave him. I obeyed.

My relationship with Erminio lasted not more than a year. As happens in the sea, where the bigger fish devour the smaller ones, Erminio, rich and important as he was, counted among his friends a man called Sirio who was a hundred times richer and more important than himself. Physically, also, Sirio was the opposite of Erminio. The latter was thickset, stout and short; the former, thin, tall, pale and slightly cadaverous. These two men confronted each other one day, under my very eyes, like two sharks at the bottom of the sea, in a business discussion of which I understood nothing except that Sirio, if he wished, could ruin Erminio at any moment. I remember the sarcastic words with which Sirio finally belaboured the speechless, defeated Erminio: 'Why, just imagine! You've made a few pennies and you think you're God knows who! But you're mistaken. Tomorrow, if I choose, you'll be reduced to rags again, running round hither and thither, worried and cringing.' Erminio did not breathe a word; I realized that he did not speak because he knew it was not advisable. Sirio rose, waved his hand in farewell and went out. With sudden decision I followed him and joined him in the hall. 'Sirio,' I said, 'you've forgotten something.'

'What?'

'Me.'

Now I am alone in Sirio's luxurious, vulgar bedroom and am looking at myself, in perplexity, in a large looking-glass. I have just woken up, I am naked, and am examining myself. Is my perplexity concerned with my body or with something else, for instance the direct, non-tortuous, in fact cynical way in which I left Erminio for Sirio? Then I suddenly understood: it was both. I was no longer the eighteen-year-old girl, provoking but ignorant, of the times of Roberto and Valerio; the mirror reflected the image of an ageless woman, with a thin body and a hard, strained expression. At the same time the vitality which once deceived me with its tortuosities, its false objectives but also its innocence, had perhaps vanished for ever. The age of physiological indolence was over. The age of simple, direct, rational calculation had begun.

UNEDUCATED

When Tullio insisted, on the telephone, that I should read the book on Che Guevara, I said to him, 'I've tried to read it but I couldn't manage it. I'm not interested in politics, I'm not interested in Latin America, I'm not interested in guerrilla warfare. Why should I read it?'

At the other end of the line, he asked, 'May one know what does interest you?'

'My own problems.'

'And what are your problems?'

'My problems are my problems and they don't concern anyone but me.'

So then he gave me a lecture, according to his usual practice. 'No one has *personal* problems except practical ones, in other words, problems which are not real problems. The only *real* problems are problems that are not *personal*, that is, the problems of art, of politics, of culture, of science and so on. The problems of things in which one is interested for love of the things themselves, without any idea of usefulness. You are not interested in anything except yourself, therefore you can't have problems.'

For some reason I was offended, and I replied, 'You talk to me in that mean way because you wanted me to go to bed with you and you didn't succeed. Goodbye.' And I threw down the receiver. I always do that when one of my many suitors has annoyed me. I throw down the receiver and don't see him again.

After this telephone conversation I turned round and saw that my mother was looking at me from the armchair in which she was sitting reading the newspaper. We are two women on our own, and we are fond of one another and we greatly resemble one another; the only difference is that my mother is thirty years older than me. We might, in fact, be a couple of sisters, one slightly wasted and worn, the other fresh and untouched. My mother smiled and then asked me, 'What are your problems?'

'When I was a child,' I replied, 'I often heard you say on the telephone, to the many men who were courting you, "My problems are my problems and they don't concern anyone but me." Forgive me, but I stole the expression from you because it applies also to myself. What are my problems? I don't know. But I have great vitality and I want to devote it to men.'

'I had the same problem, too.'

'We don't understand one another. Not to men for the purpose of making love. To men, to human beings, in order to do them good.'

Smiling (she's always smiling, for some reason), my mother admitted, 'My problem, on the other hand, as you say, was love. In my time, love was very important.'

'And did you solve this problem of love?'

'No, I was twice married, and I had prosperity and a good social position; but love—no.'

'Why?'

'I don't know why. I only know that one starts with the problem of vitality which, as you say, one wishes to devote to others. But then, instead, one ends up by solving nothing but the practical problem. I wanted love, instead of which I had only prosperity. It's nobody's fault: things are like that.'

All of a sudden, a great anger overcame me. 'In my case,' I cried, 'the fault is yours. You gave me a wrong education, from beginning to end. In this house there's never been a single book. I'm an ignoramus, I know nothing, and—what is worse—I don't manage to be interested in anything. I'm a hopeless illiterate and the fault is entirely yours.'

Smiling, perfectly calm, she replied, 'In my time, daughters were brought up in order to find good husbands. Girls did not then talk of going deeply into things. I gave you the education that was then required.'

I became even more angry, and cried, 'I don't want to go deeply into things; you're an idiot. I want to do good to humanity. But I can't do so because you brought me up in such a way that I can't manage to take an interest in anything but myself.'

'Don't call your mother an idiot.'

I shrugged my shoulders, went to my own room, put on a pair of riding-boots and a long Oriental caftan, and then went out at a run, shouting, 'I'll be out for lunch and dinner and perhaps for tonight as well. See you tomorrow morning.' As I drove my little car through the Roman traffic, I kept turning over in my mind what Tullio had said on the telephone. There was no doubt that he had spoken out of revenge because he had not succeeded in getting me to go to bed with him and, as we know, the intellectual avenges himself on the woman who rejects him by calling her an ignoramus: it's his only superiority. But it was also true that he had said things that were quite correct. I was not interested in anything, owing to the wrong education given me by my mother—not in anything beyond myself. And yet, and yet . . . I felt, at moments, that I had an immense and wonderful vitality, and I felt also that I wanted to place this vitality at the service of mankind. How could this contradiction be explained? Suddenly, as I was thinking of these things, I burst into floods of tears. The tears whipped my face like a furious shower of rain flinging itself against a window-pane. It was a beautiful day, full of sunshine, but I could hardly see for weeping. So, like a fool, I turned on the wipers, just as though my sight were dimmed not by weeping but by rain which was not really there. Amid my tears I said aloud, 'Mum, why didn't you make me, as a child, understand that the real problems are not personal, and that the personal problems are not real problems?' As can be seen, even though I had thrown down the telephone receiver when Tullio was speaking, I had learned his lesson well.

On the Via Appia I reached the villa of the actor-director for whom I worked every now and then (though I don't need to, since we are comfortably off) just to feel independent. Sometimes I may be a nude extra in a single scene of one of his 'sexy' films; sometimes I do typewriting for him (I have a diploma as a shorthand-typist) on one of his scripts. With Bob (really he is Italian and is called Roberto) I feel safe, for he would never try to get me into bed: women don't interest him.

The drive went up between two rows of flowering olean-

ders and came out to face an immense English-type lawn
surrounded with willows and cypresses. There was a swimming-pool, heart-shaped and blue, with an artificial tufa
rock down which bubbled a real waterfall. The villa, on a
single floor, was red and of the Roman farmhouse type. A
bearded man whom from a distance I did not recognize was
waving his arms as though to greet me. As I came nearer,
my heart, for some reason, gave a sudden leap: it was he,
Che Guevara, with his beret, his smiling eyes, his Christ-
like beard, his workman's blouse and his guerrilla jeans. I
got out of the car in bewilderment. Bob, for he it was, threw
out his arms and cried, 'Aren't I perfect? Am I not Che?
I'm going to shoot and act in a film about Che and you must
read all these books and extract the substance of them and
make me a report of two hundred pages from which I myself, in turn, will extract the theme. The film will be called
"Nancahuazu" from the place where Che had his camp.
We'll shoot the whole thing in the Abruzzi.' As he said this
he went over to a small table under the arcade, took up a
pile of books in his arms and went and put them, without
more ado, into my car. Disconcerted, I asked, 'But what is
all that stuff?'

'It's all stuff about Latin America.'

'But I don't know anything about either Latin America
or about anything else. I'm an ignoramus, an illiterate.'

'What school did you go to?'

'Secondary school.'

'That's all right and more than enough. Read the books
and squeeze out two hundred pages, with all the facts. Only
the facts. Time: one month. Remuneration: a million lire.
And now go away, because I'm busy. Goodbye, you lovely,
lucky creature.'

Well, I went home in a daze and immediately sat down at
my table. Strange to say, whereas Tullio, who wished me to
do things for the love of those same things, had no authority
over me, Bob, who wished me to do the same things to earn
a little money, had already persuaded and subjugated me.
Nevertheless, I was terrified at my ignorance: it was really
true, of Latin America I knew nothing at all. But as soon as

I opened the first of those books and began, methodically, to note down the 'facts'—a miracle!—I realized that everything was going marvellously well. My mind was a perfect little machine, well oiled and in a state of complete efficiency; and I hadn't known it. As I proceeded with the work, I became aware that Latin America, politically, economically, socially, historically, anthropologically, held no secrets for me. Everything was clear; everything was made up of 'facts'. And this, inexplicably, was precisely because Latin America and Che Guevara *did not interest me*.

So I worked for a month on end, on those thirty books that Bob had given me, typing the pages with greater and greater ease and less and less curiosity. The farther I advanced, the better I worked and the less I was interested. In the end I had two hundred pages with all, really all the facts. I went by car to the villa and found the entrance gates and all the doors wide open; but nobody at home. There was hot sunshine and a great silence; on the blue water of the swimming-pool floated an enormous green and yellow rubber frog. I deposited my typescript well in view on a table in the living-room; then I undressed and had a bathe in the pool, without any costume, quite naked. Then I dressed again and went back home.

A week passed and then I received a bunch of roses and an envelope. Inside the envelope was a cheque for a million and a sheet of paper with just these words, 'Well done!' So then I picked up, in one armful, the thirty books on Latin America, opened a cupboard and bundled them into it, higgledy-piggledy. At the same moment it was as though a breath of wind had blown upon my memory and swept away everything I had read during that month, in order to write the two hundred pages for Bob. Thus I went back, all at once, to being the ignoramus, the illiterate I had always been. I had forgotten everything, all in a moment. I sat down in front of the typewriter, took my face between my hands and burst into tears.

WORDS OF AN ACTRESS

After taking Strindberg's *Miss Julie* all round Italy, acting the chief part for the first time in my life, I collapsed when the company broke up. I shut myself up in my room and never left it. For my meals I made this arrangement: I took the tray handed me by my mother through the half-opened door, ate something, and then went back to bed and turned off the light again. I no longer had any wish to live; but not for any precise reason; merely because it seemed to me that living was too exhausting and I couldn't manage it any further. From time to time, opening my eyes wide in the darkness, I would whisper, 'Jesus, let me die as quickly as possible.' But I was not demoralized, or disgusted, or depressed; merely exhausted.

I thought about death, naturally; but, strange to say, I did not see this death in the future, as being faced in advance, but rather as situated back in the past, or actually *before* the past. For we stand between two deaths: from the first, we come; we go towards the second. But the first is more certain because, so to speak, we have already had the experience of it. If, in fact, death is nothingness, as I believe it to be, then I have already lived through this state of nothingness before being born and consequently it appears to me to be more reassuring and restful than the other vague, fantastic nothingness that awaits me at the end of my life. So, when I said, 'Jesus, let me die as quickly as possible', what I really meant was, 'Jesus, let me as quickly as possible go back, let me go back whence I came.' All this was not, of course, as clear in my mind as when I set it forth here. But I knew that this was more or less the sense of it.

One morning when I was lying, as usual, in the dark, huddled down in my bed, I had a fit of coughing and then a taste in my mouth like the taste of blood. You must know that, between the ages of fourteen and sixteen, I lived in a sanatorium in the mountains because I had incipient signs of tuberculosis. As soon as I became conscious of this taste, I was at once flooded with a feeling of immense joy. I would now abandon everything: the theatre, publicity, notoriety, receptions, interviews—everything; and I would return to the sanatorium, which, with pleasurable anticipation, I could already see, with its long wards, its rooms all alike, its bare windows whose panes, according to the weather, sometimes swarmed with swirling snowflakes, sometimes shone with brilliant, unreal sunlight. The word 'return', moreover, had a particular meaning for me; it was as though I wished to return to the sanatorium, not in order to be cured, but to die. But I did not in the least think that I should die physically. I knew this illness; and I was sure that once again I should escape from it. No, I felt that the death to which I aspired with so great a longing, as being the only real repose, signified dying to the new and laborious life which awaited me in the future if I came back and repeated the life I had already lived.

When, about midday, my mother as usual knocked at the door to hand me my luncheon tray through the opening, I went to open the door and said to her, 'Come in, then. I've something to say to you.'

My mother rolled (that is the right word for it: she is small, spherical and moves quickly like a ball) from the doorway to the window, and in the half-darkness I saw her take hold of the blind-cord and pull. The room was filled with the dazzling white light of the sultry sky. 'At last!' she exclaimed. 'It's a most beautiful day! Get dressed, there are lots of things to be done. Besides, during these last few days so many people have telephoned. And I'm tired of saying that you're not at home.'

I sat up on the bed; I tried to cough again; but this time I did not succeed. 'I have to tell you,' I said, 'that I'm ill and that consequently I shall have to return as soon as possible to the sanatorium.'

'What d'you mean, you're ill? What's the matter with you?'

'I've been spitting blood. Evidently it's come back again.'

'But that's not possible. The X-rays showed that you were completely cured.'

'We'll get the X-rays done again and it'll be seen that I've had a relapse.'

'But what are you saying? It's not possible.'

'It's so entirely possible that in a short time I shall telephone to the sanatorium to book a room.'

'Wait a moment; what's the matter with you? Who's been getting at you? How d'you come to be so certain?'

'I feel it. Besides, I saw the blood. What more d'you want?'

She looked at me and I looked at her. And then I hated the expression of disappointment on her round face with its tiny features which were made smaller, so to speak, by its plumpness, and I thought, 'It tells its own story, d'you want to see how?'

'What a misfortune!' she said. 'Just now, when . . .'

'When what?'

'Well, when you were reaping the fruits of so many efforts.'

'What fruits, what efforts?'

'When your talent as an actress was at last being recognized.'

'Why, what talent?'

'Would you now deny even that you have any talent?'

'Even admitting that I have, what does it matter?'

'What d'you mean, what does it matter? It matters more than anything.'

'To you, not to me.'

'You were beginning to make a name for yourself, to be somebody; people were already speaking of you as a safe promise for the Italian theatre, and all of a sudden, there we are: everything has to be done over again. And what a misfortune for me! This was really uncalled for.'

We looked at one another again in silence. Then suddenly I understood perfectly clearly that the subject of the conversation between mother and myself was not my illness. That taste of blood during my fit of coughing was certainly not of tubercular origin: I was sure of it. No, the subject between my mother and me was the fact of living and of having the wish to live. I did not have the wish to live; the sanatorium to which I wanted to return was in reality the womb of my mother from which she had ejected me of necessity when, as is said so appropriately, she brought me to the light. I myself detested that same light with my whole soul; and this was the explanation of my longing for the pristine darkness. Instead of saying to her, 'Get me back to the sanatorium', I should have said, 'Get me back inside you, in fact even farther back, to the nothingness that I was before you conceived me.'

It is indeed good to say things like this to a woman like my mother. In fact, to any mother. I remained silent for a little; then I asked her, 'Will you tell me what you thought when I was born?'

'What d'you mean?'

'The birth of a child is, after all, the result of a wish. One wishes or one does not wish to bring a child into the world. You wished it, didn't you?'

'But what's that got to do with it, now?'

'Answer me to the point: you wanted me to be born?'

'Certainly. Of course. I wanted it and your father wanted it. You were our first child. When you were born, we were both of us happy.'

'Good. And I myself, when I was born, did I seem to you happy to be born?'

'What the devil are you talking about?'

'Answer my question: did I look as if I was happy when I was born? Did I laugh, did I clap my hands and look round me with joy and admiration? Or—as is more probable—did I cry and complain bitterly?'

The question left her open-mouthed. Finally she admitted unwillingly, 'Of course, as everybody knows, babies come into the world crying. But you, the very moment you were born, had an extraordinary loud voice which proclaimed your vitality.'

'Or, on the other hand, shall we say that it proclaimed my despair?'

All of a sudden my mother, as usual, burst into tears. She remained motionless, her face bespotted with big tears as

round as herself, as though someone had thrown a bucketful
of water over her. Then I burst out laughing, nervously, and
pulled back the bed-clothes and jumped out of bed, ex-
claiming, 'Don't you understand that I wanted to have a
joke? Don't you know that actors are always pretending,
even in life? I'm perfectly well and you mustn't believe what
I say. Words of an actress, Mum, words of an actress!'

WOMAN...HORSE

As I was getting out of the car, in the blinding midday sultriness, someone whom I did not see said to me, 'You're like a big horse', as he passed close beside me. I went indoors; my parents were already at table and I could see them through the glass door; and I went straight to my room and hastily undressed to take a shower. Naked, I climbed into the bath, which was yellow with age, took hold of the old-fashioned hand-douche and directed its meagre jet on to my body. There was an oblong looking-glass right opposite the bath; and as I sprayed myself I could see my entire person.

As I looked at myself, the words 'big horse' recurred in my mind and I could not but recognize the truth of them. I am in fact very tall, with broad shoulders and a wide pelvis; but I have long, agile, thin legs; and, in general, the big feminine machine of my body gives an impression of harmony and even of elegance. Precisely, in fact, like that of a horse; for horses are the only animals which are at the same time both large and graceful. But alas, my bony face, too, is horse-like, with its very low forehead, long nose and prominent mouth. However it is above all my eyes that are reminiscent of those of a horse. Round, black, limpid, they nevertheless display a senseless uneasiness in the depths of their limpidity.

At this point I began to wonder whether the unknown passer-by who had called me a 'big horse' had intended to pay me a compliment. And I decided that all he had intended was a description of me. But indeed it is so: I am a 'big horse', a girl who, if she had got married, might perhaps now be merely a matron; but who, instead, by remaining unmarried, had gradually turned into a caricature of herself and had ended up by resembling an animal.

The idea of the horse came back to me shortly afterwards, when I was sitting at table. My father put out his hand to give me a pat and I immediately jerked my head violently away, just like a horse. My mother suddenly addressed me,

'Rossana'; and I, at the mention of my name, gave a start, exactly like a horse shying. My mother then asked me, 'Why, what's the matter with you? What are you thinking about?'

I was thinking that I hated my parents and that I felt I could no longer go on living with them. But I was also thinking that they had never done me any harm and that I was unhappy with them merely because they were happy and their happiness excluded me.

This happiness needs to be clearly understood. Perhaps it would be more correct to say that they have succeeded in creating a kind of balance between them, a relationship, as it were, of parts that complement each other. Truly each one of them could say of the other, in middle-class parlance, 'This is my better half.' Unfortunately, however, the whole that these two halves comprise is not of the most amiable. And so, in myself, to the feeling of exclusion is added that of rebellion.

Here is a picture of my father: a flabby, swollen face, light blue eyes with a fatuous expression in them, a bulbous nose, a greedy mouth, fair hair going grey but still curly and always dishevelled. His whole person expresses an impudent and utterly repugnant sensuality. And now my mother. She is older than my father; she might be his aunt or an elder sister. In her angular thinness, in her crazy severity, there is not even one single drop of the sensuality which so disgusts me in my father. This also is repugnant to me. It is not right to be either as sensual as my father or as little sensual as my mother.

Then something happened which set off the mechanism of my parents' happiness. The maid whom my mother had taken on about ten days before came into the room. I was struck, once again, by the 'unsuitableness' of this woman, which however, when considered from the point of view of my father and my mother, was quickly changed, magically, into 'suitableness'. Mature and striking in appearance, she had dyed hair of an ugly, coppery red, with one loose lock that hung continually over a motionless, fateful eye. She was small, almost deformed, with a prominent bosom and behind; she sought to correct this natural obscenity by the ridiculous and vulgar haughtiness of her bearing. She served us with the air of one who was doing a job not her own and which she despised, holding out the tray at a dangerous angle and turning away her head, as much as to say, 'Come on, hurry up, I'm waiting.' My father's eyes followed her in every movement; and my mother's eyes followed my father's. Then the woman handed the tray to my father and he, placing his hand on the table, contrived lightly to touch *her* hand. My mother said quietly, 'One doesn't touch the maid's hand.' My father helped himself and, as though nothing had happened, began eating in silence.

Why do I say they were happy? Because they uphold one another. My father's sensuality justifies my mother's moralism in the same way that the latter justifies my father's sensuality. Sometimes I wonder how things were at the beginning, how this unbreakable equilibrium came about, and I don't arrive at any solution. It may be that there was sensuality and that the moralism arose from it as a reaction; but perhaps, on the contrary, there was moralism and sensuality broke away from it as a relief. Anyhow the partnership between my mother who represses and my father who is repressed, works well. This is proved, if in no other way, by the fact that, in spite of my numerous attempts to share in the family life, I have always felt myself, over the years, to be slyly excluded.

I thought of these things with bowed head in front of my untouched plate, without eating. Then again I had a horse-like impulse. I saw the maid walking across the room and my father following her movements with a furtive glance. My mother said in a low voice, 'Eyes front!' I put my napkin down on the table, muttered that I was not hungry, jumped up hastily and went to my room.

I threw myself on the bed and waited impatiently until my parents had shut themselves up in their own room for their afternoon rest. As I waited I did not think of anything; I was merely an astonished witness of the incoherent tumult in my mind. At last, as soon as I was sure they were asleep, I rang the bell.

There was a knock. 'Come in,' I said; and the maid stood in the doorway without coming in, leaning in a familiar, listless way against the doorpost. 'Margherita,' I said, 'do you realize that things can't go on like this?'

Unexpectedly, she at once agreed with me. 'I know, but will you tell me what I can do about it?'

'Give notice.'

'I've already tried four times. But your mother clasped her hands and begged me not to go. So I've stayed.'

'Now tell me the truth: did my mother persuade you to stay by offering you a very big increase in wages?'

'Well, yes, but what ought I to have done? Refuse?'

'I'm not saying that.'

'Then I ask you again: what ought I to do, with your father laying hands on me at every possible moment, and your mother who, in order to make me stay, pays me twice as much as anyone else?'

My horse-like craziness now rose in revolt. Almost without thinking, I said, 'Tell my father that it's all right by you, on condition that he leaves my mother and goes to live with you.'

I saw her give me a look of genuine surprise. Fundamentally she was a person of common sense and there were certain things she did not understand. Slowly she asked, 'And is it really you who are making me a suggestion of that kind?'

'In any case, ask to come and eat at our table, as a member of the family by right.'

Margherita did not appreciate my extravagant ideas. She murmured in a mumbling sort of way, 'What a family!'; then she went slowly away, leaving the door half open.

When I was alone I went over to the window and looked out, stupefied, into the street. We live in Via Nazionale, on the first floor of an old house. Four rows of cars, two going in one direction and two in the other, were advancing slowly in an atmosphere dimmed by oppressive heat and petrol fumes. Amongst all these cars an old horse-drawn cab was proceeding in a dignified manner. How strange the horse seemed in the midst of all these machines! How curious its tall, big body on its four thin legs! And how clearly one could see that it was restlessly champing at the bit, unable to insinuate itself into the mechanized traffic! I watched it with a fascinated, fraternal feeling. The words 'big horse' evidently continued to have an effect. I said to myself that I was an 'unmanageable horse'; and as I looked at the cab moving away very slowly amongst the cars, I began to weep, standing at the window-sill, sticking out my lips to catch the tears, just as a horse sticks out its mouth to grasp a lump of sugar.

DEEP SOUTH

A marvellous summer! A divine summer! I was in one of my 'good' periods and I was, as they say, beside myself with the frenzied joy of living. I am rather short, with an enormous bosom, a long, pale face, smooth hair; insignificant, in fact. Well, during that summer the joy of living had even transformed me physically. My hair had become electric; my eyes like those of one possessed; my face red and fiery. I even felt I was tall. And as for my bosom, usually my greatest affliction, why, I tossed it about hither and thither, coming very near to making a display of it. Unforgettable summer! I slept alternately either at Marco's or at Bernardo's; we would wake up at eleven, make our efficient telephone calls to rally our group of friends; then off we would go to the sea, in two or three cars, all of us boys and girls of the same age. At the seaside we would get into a motor-boat and, in the twinkling of an eye, were far out from the shore. There we did all sorts of things: complete nudism, diving, water-skiing, under-water fishing. Naked, one on top of the other, we basked in the sun to the point of utter stupefaction. We ate a few sandwiches and then went back to Rome in time to clean ourselves up and go and have supper in some *pizzeria* or snack-bar. Immediately afterwards, off we would rush to a night-club—the best moment of the day. What joy! What frenzy! I danced and danced and danced. With the overwhelming din of numbers of electric guitars heightened by loudspeakers, I would end by losing my head. I would take off my shoes, my sweater, my skirt and dance all alone, in my slip and bra, surrounded by a circle of hand-clapping admirers, until the usual doorkeeper chased the whole lot of us out into the street. That summer we had a special liking for fountains. As soon as we came out of the night-club, at about four in the morning, we would go and throw ourselves into one of the many fountains of Rome, the Barcaccia in Piazza di Spagna, the

Trevi fountain, the fountains in Piazzi Navona, the basin in Piazza Barberini. Sometimes we finished up at the police station. More often, soaking wet, our clothes sticking to our bodies, we would go and lie down, all of us together, now in one house, now in another. Oh, what a lovely summer!

With the end of the summer my 'good' period also came to an end; the 'bad' period began. The group dispersed and I left for my own home, in the South, where my family, very rich, very noble and very degenerate, own feudal domains as big as provinces. The South! Talk of the South! Sometimes, with regard to the South in the United States, I have come across the expression in the newspapers, the 'Deep South'. Rubbish! The really deep, really submerged South is my own. One cannot go deeper than that, it must be said, without dying. At any rate, I myself should die! This is the degree of depth, in terms of the journey: first the motorway, full of cars; then a secondary road, asphalted but less frequented; then a minor road, still asphalted but almost empty; then a crushed stone road, our own road, across our property. Bare hills, bare valleys, the whole region devoted to corn-growing; and, along the road, peasants saluting. Finally an earth track and at the end of it, on a bald hill, the villa. As I went gradually along, I felt I was becoming short again, with an enormous bust, straight hair and small pale face: insignificant. My 'bad' period was beginning again, no mistake about it.

The villa was like a huge crab, with two curving projections forming the two claws of the crab and, farther back, the baroque main door, forming the crab's mouth. A crab? Perhaps more like a scorpion than a crab! When the majordomo, in his working jacket and with a three-day beard, bowed and kissed my hand and called me 'Excellency', I asked in a faint voice where my grandmother was and then moved away towards the front door because my grandmother had come out and was walking towards me gesticulating. The slovenly old hag, with a nose like a pirate and moustaches to match, a princess and a duchess with endless titles, embraced me and shouted, 'You've arrived just in time for dinner. There's *pasta al forno*!' My grandmother always

shouts, habitually, even if, let us suppose, she has to say,
'Don't bawl, speak quietly.' I did not listen to her; in complete silence I went straight up to my room, an immense
room with four windows on the façade and a canopied bed,
where I undressed at once and got into bed. 'I should like
to die,' I thought, 'yes, to die, to die, to die, not to go on
living.' That was how my 'bad' period began. Lying now on
top of the bed-clothes, now underneath them, I spent two
months in bed, inert, my arms dangling loose, my eyes fixed
on the windows through which I saw the sky, always, every
day, a 'mackerel' sky: the sky of my 'bad' periods. I wept
continuously and felt I did not wish to go on living, that I
wanted to die.

One day my grandmother, shouting as usual, thrust into
my room a young man of uncommon beauty and then went
away. He was a distant relation of mine; he had said to my
grandmother, 'Eleonora is not well? I'll see to that'; and
now there he was, standing in front of me. Handsome, extremely handsome, fair-haired, with intensely expressive,
almost frenzied, light blue eyes, a solid, healthy, pink and
white face, a small fair moustache, a red mouth. His name
was Corrado, and he was lively, extremely lively, elated,
over-excited. 'Come on, get out of bed!' he cried; 'life is
awaiting us!' And he compelled me to rise and follow him.
We went for a drive. As he drove, he talked continuously; he
had an enormously wide culture, especially in the matter of
ruins, monuments and museums; and I, in spite of feeling
like a worn-out rag, could not help listening to him, fascinated. I'm as ignorant as a goat; but culture impresses me,
especially if presented with such fire and such vivacity as
did Corrado. That day we visited a couple of castles and a
museum.

Corrado knew everything; he had written a number of
monographs on monuments, which he then published at his
own expense. He was enthusiastic about kings and queens
and historical characters; about Christians and Turks; about
stones, paintings, statues. In the museum, the custodian left
us alone and then, after a caress and a kiss, a kiss and a
caress, what with one thing and another, given his over-

flowing vitality and my own deathly inertia, the thing that
was bound to happen, happened. And just imagine where!
On a historic bed in one of the rooms of the museum, a bed
covered in faded plum-coloured velvet with four silken ropes
round it, the bed of some king or queen belonging to our
part of the country. The custodian, obviously paid by Corrado, did not put in an appearance; in the end I was exhausted, inert, corpse-like, and I said to him, 'Now listen,
leave me here, on this historic bed. Go away. Tomorrow
morning they'll find me dead and it's all the same whether I
die in a museum or in my own home: it makes no difference.' But just imagine! He burst into a great fit of laughter,
with that very beautiful mouth and perfect teeth, forced me
to get off the bed, and thus it was that our love affair began.
A love affair between a worn-out human rag like me and a
monster of vitality like him. A love affair which took us
round perpetually to castles, museums, towers, palaces, ruins.
I followed behind him repeating that I wanted to die and he
would answer me with those great bursts of laughter that
shook his healthful cheeks, saying that on the contrary I
must go on living, if not for my own sake, at any rate for his.

In the end we decided to move together to Rome. We left
by car and it was I who drove. Gradually, as I extricated myself from the Deep South, from the earth track to the minor
road, from that to the secondary road, from the secondary
road to the motorway, I felt that my 'bad' period was fading
away; and my 'good' period began to make itself felt. The
sky was no longer a 'mackerel' sky; it was full of numberless
white and golden clouds. I became more and more elated,
so that I even forgot Corrado. Then his silence—he who was
usually such a chatterbox—made me suspicious. As I drove,
I gave him a sidelong glance. I very nearly failed to recognize him: slumped in his seat, deflated, flabby, his eyes half-
closed, on his face and in the whole attitude of his body
there was an expression, well-known to me, of cruel distress.
I asked him what was wrong. He replied in a faint voice,
'Don't worry. It's my bad period. It's coming on, I can feel
it. It's nothing. It lasts for a short time and then it passes.'

'How long does it last?'

'Oh well, last time I was in bed for two months.'

In Rome we went to an hotel. As soon as I reached the bed-room, I went to the telephone to collect the group. Corrado, on the other hand, threw himself fully dressed on the bed. That same evening I went out to dinner and on to a night-club with the group; but Corrado did not want to come and remained on the bed. There I found him, in the same posi-tion, at five in the morning, when I came home again. I had to undress him as he could not manage it by himself; then slip on his pyjamas; and finally I had actually to arrange his legs and arms and head for him to go to sleep—just as though he were a marionette with broken springs.

It was thus that our life in Rome began: I myself, out all the time, always elated, always in good form; and Corrado all the time lying on the bed, either underneath or on top of the bed-clothes, inert, gazing at the ceiling, his arms lying limp. I tried to revive him but without much diligence be-cause I recognized in him my own trouble and knew from experience that there was nothing to be done. It was a cyclical question, as with me; he went from elation to de-pression, as I did. Unfortunately, however, his periods of depression coincided with my periods of elation and *vice versa*; and so we did not even have the comfort of suffering together, after having rejoiced together. But I was very fond of him, he had been my first love affair, and so I remained faithful to him, even if I spent the evenings and nights with other men. I loved him so much, I shared in his distress and identified myself so closely with it that, in the end, in a moment of supreme elation, on an occasion when he had feebly repeated to me, 'Oh, I've no longer any wish to live, I want to die, to die, to die; Oh God, let me die as soon as pos-sible,' I cried out, 'Let us die together. You will die because you hate life; I shall die because I have a passionate love of living. And thus your horror of life and my joy in living will be merged in the same death.'

It was late at night and I had only just come back from the night-club where I had been dancing for five hours on end; Corrado shook his head; his depression prevented him from coming to any decision. So we both lay down, each in his own bed. There was a bedside table, with a bottle of water and phials of sleeping pills between the two beds.

I fell asleep at once, feeling happy and full of life. All of a sudden a sound of groping on the little table awoke me. I put out my hand in the dark and encountered Corrado's hand; he was pouring an entire phial of barbiturates into the glass. Still feeling elated, I said to him, 'Well done; give me the glass, I'll drink half of it and you can drink the other half.' He said nothing, but handed me the glass and I drank half of the water and then gave him back the glass. Immediately I plunged into a deathly sleep.

I awoke two days later in a hospital room. My grandmother was at my bedside and she shouted at me, 'At last you've woken up. God be praised!' I could not understand at all; my grandmother went on shouting, 'Fancy wanting to die because someone or other called Corrado leaves you and goes back to his own home and his own people! What came over you? He runs away by car and you immediately swallow a big glass of barbiturates. One sees how young you are! But the world is full of Corrados. For every Corrado lost, there are a hundred others to be found.' Do you see what had happened? Corrado had changed his mind; he had not taken the pills, but instead had left by car for his own South, his own Deep South, where castles, museums, ruins and monographs awaited him. At this moment he was no doubt already bursting with vitality; he was already beside himself with euphoria. As I have said, in spite of the abortive suicide which in any case was brought about by love and by an exuberant joy of life, I found myself in one of my 'good' periods. And so I suddenly started laughing and laughing and laughing. Then I said to my grandmother, who was staring at me in astonishment, 'From now onwards, I'm for Rome and Corrado can stay down there in his own country.'

LADY GODIVA

My husband idealized me, but this gave me no pleasure, in fact, to be quite frank, it annoyed me. Admittedly I am an attractive, perhaps even a beautiful, woman, with my small, muscular, energetic physique, my strong face softened by its dark blue eyes, my mass of thick fair hair; but at the age of twenty-five, what woman is not attractive? Admittedly I have a passion for all kinds of sport, am a good swimmer, a more than passable horsewoman, an expert skier; but I am not the only one, the sporting type of woman is quite common today. My husband, on the other hand, looked upon me as a rarity, as a unique case; and in his obstinate brain my attractiveness and my sporting abilities became fused together to form a positively ideal picture, in which I was absolutely unable to recognize myself.

Besides, in marriage everything should be reciprocal, even idealization. But whereas my husband idealized me, I did not idealize him, not in the very least. I saw him as he was: unfortunate in his physical appearance (there was something of the sacristan about him : a plump, greasy face, a foolish smile, the short-sightedness of a mole; half-hearted in his so-called studies (Etruscan archaeology and psychoanalysis; he had been scribbling for years, but nothing had ever come of it); and with an unsound quality inherited from his family (an old family, minor nobility from the Maremma region, full of eccentrics and worthless characters and madmen).

Sometimes, when he got too much on my nerves, I would shout out the truth to his face, 'D'you know why you see me as I am *not*? Why you idealize me? Because you live on the income from your estate and don't work. Because you spend the whole day idling and idleness always ends by making people lose the sense of reality, by inspiring people with morbid thoughts. Yes, because there's something morbid in your way of looking at me. I am not what you think I am.

I'm a sporting, rather pretty young woman, that's all. And don't idealize me, either, as a character. Since I was poor and wanted to be rich, I married you for your money, without loving you. D'you see?'

Now would you believe it? This crude sincerity had no effect upon him whatever. All he said was that it did not matter so much to him to be loved as to love. And then, in a transport of this aforesaid love, he actually went so far as to throw himself at my feet and kiss my cowhide boots which, together with leather-patched trousers and a checked shirt, formed my habitual costume in the country, that is, almost always.

Lady Godiva! How my husband wearied my ears with the legend of this noble lady of many centuries ago who, to relieve the poverty of the peasants oppressed by the crushing taxes imposed by her husband, consented to ride on horseback through the streets of Coventry clothed in nothing but her hair! My husband said that I resembled her in every point because, being small and possessed of an enormous mass of hair, I would be able, like Lady Godiva, to clothe myself in my hair. He even went so far, in moments of tenderness, as to call me Godiva instead of Paola, which is my name. But the resemblance did not exist. I am not of noble origin (I am the daughter of a railway signalman): I have never had any liking for peasants: I know them too well; and finally I am not in the smallest degree an exhibitionist. For no one will persuade me that this Godiva, in showing herself naked on horseback, was not demonstrating her own taste.

But he could never get rid of his obsession with Lady Godiva because, as I have said, he lived in idleness and thus had the whole day to ponder over his oddities. So much so that he finally made a suggestion to me: to give him pleasure, I must one day mount my horse quite naked and allow him to admire me as I rode slowly round the open space in front of our villa, possibly at night and in full moonlight. This mad suggestion he stammered out with difficulty, with a bewildered smile and a sort of sparkle in his eyes behind his thick lenses. We were sitting at table and I immediately told him indignantly and frankly what I thought, 'You know what it shows, this fixation of yours to make me act Lady Godiva? That you're a *voyeur*! Yes, you're a *voyeur*, a Peeping Tom—of a special kind, if you like—but a *voyeur* just the same.'

He did not bat an eyelid; when castigated, he was a veritable rhinoceros. Then, after a few days, he insisted again, this time, however, attacking me on my weak side, my passion for horses. In the same stuttering way, with the same bewildered smile and the same sparkle in his eye, he told me that, if I performed this parade on horseback in the manner of Lady Godiva, he would make me a present of a Hungarian thoroughbred which we had seen together, a month earlier, during a trip we had made to Hungary, in a famous stud farm in that country. It cost fifty thousand florins, that is, about a million lire. A good price for a little ride on horseback in the moonlight.

So I agreed, albeit with anger and repugnance. We went back to Hungary, to the stud farm two hundred kilometres from Budapest. And I, with a sudden leap of the heart, saw again the desolate plain beneath the immense sky and the narrow openings for the hurdles in the riding-grounds and the long, low buildings of the stables with their close-set embrasures. Trembling with joy, I re-entered one of the stables, no longer as a visitor but as a buyer. And it was as a buyer that I examined one by one, in the delicious smell of fresh dung, of straw, of leather and of hay, the rows of wonderful horses in their boxes, with their heads in their mangers and their tails turned towards us. Horses to take one's breath away, fiery brown, dappled grey, black, white. I pretended to look at them one by one, minutely; but in my own heart I had already made my choice, ever since my first visit: a male five-year-old, of a silky white with a golden sheen, and with a long, flowing tail and a broad, thick, champagne-coloured mane. And with strange, bright, almost red eyes: possibly it was an albino. When I had a trial ride on it and passed and re-passed in front of my husband, myself small, very small indeed, on this great, powerful horse, for the first time his ecstatic way of looking at me scarcely annoyed me any more. So great was my joy that it almost seemed to me that I was fond of him or, at any rate, that I found his strange manner of loving me to be just and endurable.

Well, we went back to Italy; the horse arrived from Hungary; my husband said nothing but I knew that he was anxiously awaiting the night of full moon during which I should be, for a few minutes, just as he imagined me in his intellectual–*voyeur* dreams. Cunningly, however, I avoided mentioning my promise; it pleased me to keep him in suspense. Meanwhile my passion for the Hungarian thoroughbred raged irresistibly. Secretly I went time after time into the stable, and, having locked the door, I would stand there looking at him in his box, fascinated. I looked at him because he was beautiful; but above all because this beauty made me obtuse and stupid and I wanted to fathom its meaning, and did not succeed.

The moon in the clear sky of June was first of all a curved edge, then a sickle, then a corroded slice, and at last, at the height of its fullness, a dazzling silver disc. One night we went out into the open space which was white in the moonlight, with the front of the villa brightly shining and the ilexes and cypresses black and motionless all round; and I told my husband to wait for me, and I would go and fetch the horse and ride round the open space clothed only in my hair, like his Lady Godiva. He nodded, more stunned and bewildered than ever; and I went to the stable and approached the Hungarian horse's box. Yet again, as I was on the point of saddling him and leading him out, I felt the same enchantment in contemplating him, hardly able to believe that he was so beautiful; and then, when I could not have enough of observing the bright blond colouring of his mane and tail, the smooth, taut whiteness of his hindquarters, the graceful, elegant arrogance of his sturdy hooves, bent slightly at the fetlocks, when I forgot, as I gazed at him, why I was there at that unaccustomed hour, I realized, all of a sudden, that I was doing with the horse just what my husband did with me: I was idealizing him, transforming him into a creature of dreams. Thus I too was not the practical, rational person I had always claimed to be; I too was crazy, just like my husband.

At this thought I clenched my teeth in anger; then, with an almost painful effort of will, I took down the saddle from its hook and placed it on the horse. Then I undressed. I took off my shirt, my trousers, my other garments, and was left in nothing but my boots. And now my hair. I wore it knotted into a huge bun on my neck; I loosened it and it fell, reaching right down to my loins. The horse, excited, perhaps, by these preparations, turned his head to look at me as I approached him, naked and booted, and uttered a long, strange whinnying sound, as much as to say, 'You're beautiful too.' I unhitched him, took him by the bridle and led him out of the stable into the open space.

My husband was standing there, in the middle of the space, in an awkward, bewildered attitude. Walking slowly and leading the horse by the bridle, I approached him. The moonlight fell full upon me; I even had a momentary feeling of shame; but after all what did it matter? The person who was looking at me was only my husband. I handed him the bridle; mounted into the saddle with a single leap; and then started riding slowly round and round the open space. At first the horse was refractory and nervous, reared a little and caracoled; I tried to calm him, using the device of kissing him and of tapping him gently on his neck with the palm of my hand; in the end I managed to slow him down to walking pace though he was still strangely impatient and seemingly ill-intentioned. I continued to circle round the open space; my husband stood in the middle of it and turned to look at me as I went round him. Behind me my hair spread out over the saddle; in front it fell in two parallel waves over my breasts and covered my belly. I circled round once, then a second time, then a third time, still at the same slow pace, as if on parade. Then suddenly I noticed that the horse was shortening the circles round my husband, like the eddies of a whirlpool steadily withdrawing towards its centre. I tried to correct the movement of the horse and almost deceived myself into thinking I had succeeded; but somehow or other, at the seventh round I suddenly found myself dangerously close behind my husband: I was almost touching him with the toe of my boot. I pulled at the reins to get away; but just at that moment the horse reared, rose on his hind legs, straightened up more and more, remained for a very long moment towering up in an almost vertical position and then threw himself down with all his weight on top of my husband who had no time to move aside. I managed to get the horse under control at once, with relative ease, which almost surprised me; but then I understood. Assuredly the horse had had the intention of rearing in this fatal manner from the very moment when I had led him out of the stable. Now that my husband was lying motionless in the middle of the open space, the horse, having attained its purpose, had calmed down and was gently pawing the ground, scraping the gravel with his hoof.

ALLERGIC

The political discussion between my brother and our step-father became one of almost intolerable harshness. But what made it particularly unpleasant for me was my brother's obvious conviction that I was on his side against our step-father, if only because we belong (I am twenty-three and he is twenty-two) to the same generation.

I am a girl of great and conspicuous beauty who has very quickly learnt—forced to it, more or less, by masculine admiration—to keep silent as far as my mouth is concerned and to allow the other parts of my body to speak in their own mute language. Thus my brother has never come to know that, during his bitter discussions which, among other things, are made even more disagreeable because they always occur at table during meals, I am not by any means on his side but on that of our step-father. He has never come to know this because not merely am I careful not to let it leak out, but also because, infatuated as he is, he has never condescended to inquire into my opinions and my sympathies. If he had done so, he would have discovered that there is not a single one of his so-called problems about which I agree with him. To put it briefly, he has the innate temperament of a revolutionary. I myself, on the other hand, secretly and, so to speak, physiologically, am a conservative.

Why do I say 'physiologically'? Because my reaction to everything that smells of revolt and destruction does not seem to arise from my mind, which most of the time is inert and empty, but from my body, which, it must be believed, appears to be lined with nerves and muscles endowed with—how shall I say?—an acute sensibility, social, political and ideological. My brother's revolutionary attitudes, in fact, affect me not so much in my understanding as in my belly and stomach; not so much in my thought which does not react but in my skin which turns into goose-flesh, in my arms and legs which become rigid, in my bowels which contract. All this, in short, is too strong for me; and when, at table, I feel myself attacked by this physiological irritation, I seek to disguise it by tightening my legs and my elbows, straightening my bust and lowering my eyes. The somewhat convulsive character of my attitude of reserve does not escape my brother. But he is deceived, and attributes it to the conflict in my mind between sympathy for his ideas and the respect I owe to our mother's husband.

It is curious that, during these controversies, I have noticed that, whereas even the most extreme of my brother's arguments leave me indifferent, what I may call my 'muscular' conservatism contracts violently, like Galvani's frogs, as soon as certain words are uttered in a tone that is less than respectful. Even more curiously, I am aware that the significance of these words is not in any way the starting-point of my bodily reactions; it is, rather, their sound, as happens with music and, in general, with all noises. To make a comparison, what happens to me with such words is rather like what happens to some people with strawberries to which they are allergic. For some mysterious reason their bodies do not tolerate them; as soon as they have eaten them, their skins are indeed covered with red, itching pimples.

Let us take, for example, the word 'family'. To tell the truth the family, as a social reality, means nothing to me. I do not like family life. I would say that, in the family, the most offensive sincerities alternate all too often with the most hermetically concealed hypocrisies. Moreover I have, unfortunately, a fatal inclination to impose upon families by falling in love with married men and causing them to fall in love with me. At twenty-three I have already had four such anti-family intrigues, as I may call them, with the result that the families whom I have encountered have never afterwards been the same. My fate, in short—so it seems—is to bring corruption and division into organized family structures through my irresistible beauty (it is not I myself who described it in that way but the fathers of families who were charmed by me), a beauty which frightens me, even more than my lovers, as a destructive force the total, uncontrollable power of which is recognized. And yet, and

yet . . . It is only necessary for someone to utter the word
'family' with contempt, with irony, with hostile intention, it
is only necessary for the sound of this word to reach my
ear emphasized by a tone of blasphemy, for me to feel a
contraction of horror that stiffens my body from head to
foot. Contrariwise, this same word pronounced with respect,
with sympathy, with affection, relaxes that same body with
an emotion that is both edifying and afflicting and exalted.

One day at lunch the now habitual argument broke out
between my brother and my step-father. I sat silent, as usual,
even though I was secretly on the side of my step-father
whose ideas stimulated my appetite, in the customary physiological way, far more than those of my brother. I must
observe, at this point, that I do not cherish any special feelings of liking, still less of attraction, towards my step-
father. As he becomes heated and loud-voiced, I look at him
and feel that his too-fluffy curls in which the blond is turning to grey and his too-conspicuous blue eyes that always
look slightly excited, convey the idea of a maturity very
like the excessively overblown look of roses on the eve of the
final shedding of their petals. On the other hand I have a
feeling of sincere admiration for my brother, thinking of
him, without a crumb of envy but with a certain sadness,
that he is more intelligent than I am and above all more
capable of expressing this intelligence in words; whereas I
myself, mentally muted, am forced to be expressive solely
with my body.

The discussion became violent; the maid was trotting like
a frightened mouse round the table, with her tray which
everyone refused; I tightened my lips and my legs and kept
my eyes fixed on my plate. Then our mother, with the usual
inopportuneness of a senile, socially-minded woman, said
the one thing she ought not to have said. Turning towards
my brother, she exclaimed, 'Do at least remember that
you're not in public but with your family.'

Carried away by passion, my brother replied, 'I don't care
a damn about the family.'

Then something happened which I myself cannot explain
in a satisfactory way. While my brother's remark made me

freeze and stiffen all over, I suddenly felt some sort of irresistible need to make my stepfather understand that I was on his side and shared his ideas. Anyone else in my position would have spoken, thus finally dissipating a misunderstanding that had lasted too long. I, on the other hand, did an unforeseen, absurd, unforgivable thing: I stretched out my leg under the table and pressed my step-father's foot with my own. I swear that my sole desire at that moment was to let him know that I agreed with him; but I immediately became aware that he attributed a different meaning to my gesture. I saw this from the sudden reddening of his already red face; from the strange, blank and as it were confused tone of voice with which he replied to my brother, 'I forbid you to talk like that in my house.'

'In your house?'

'Yes, in my house!'

The usual consequences ensued: my brother rose and went out, banging the door behind him; I pursued him to make him come back to the table, but this time I felt that there was a falseness in my role as peacemaker. In any case my brother would not yield. He embraced me and said, 'I know that you think as I do', and went out. I went back to the living-room and the meal finished in silence.

Afterwards my step-father lay in an armchair and smoked with an air of absorption and nervousness; my mother, who had risen at twelve, declared that she felt tired and was going to 'rest'. I went to my room, slipped on a coat of some kind and, without either combing my hair or putting on any make-up, hurriedly left the house, passing through the living-room in which my step-father still lingered in his armchair.

It was half past two, the hour of siesta, of satiety, of somnolence. We live in an avenue of big plane-trees, which at this season were thick with buds. Later, in two or three hours' time, the prostitutes would be arriving in the avenue and their clients in cars; but at that moment there was nobody, neither passers-by nor cars. I walked slowly and listlessly, stooped down to pick a long blade of grass and put it between my teeth. I thrust my hands deep down into my coat pockets to pull the coat closer to my sides. Then I stopped to fasten my belt and as I did so, I looked back over my shoulder. I counted the trunks of eight plane-trees between the door of my home and myself. My step-father, who was following me, had already reached the fourth. I slackened my step.

LIFE ON THE TELEPHONE

I have moved house, because an ambassador in office may perhaps have need of a large house; but his widow has not: on the day of her husband's death she loses ninety per cent not merely of her so-called acquaintances but also of her friends. Add to this that I do not have a large family; I have only a daughter. So I moved without regret from the ten-room apartment in which I have lived with my husband to a small, elegant but confined flat of four rooms. Among the things that I took with me from my old dwelling-place was a painting, which I hung in my sitting-room. I want to describe it; for certain things to be understood, I think this is necessary. In it can be seen a woman standing beside a gilt console-table; a very beautiful woman, but with a haughty, crazy, overstrung, worldly type of beauty; made-up and attired to perfection, in a black evening dress with few but valuable jewels.

Now this woman was myself, still only a few years ago, when I was the wife of an ambassador and living in the capital of a foreign land.

I started living a quiet life, too quiet indeed, for very soon it became quietly insufferable. As a comparison, I felt rather like a soldier coming home at the end of a war. His whole life, hitherto, has been organized for one single purpose, war, which demands courage, sobriety, harshness, discipline. But now, at home, he realizes that in civilian life these qualities are of no use. Then, almost without becoming conscious of it, he begins to disarm himself, dismantling his warlike trappings one after the other. Except that the soldier goes, one fine day, to an employment agency and finds some sort of a job. But I? I was by now fifty-five years old and all I had to look forward to was an empty, solitary old age.

As though that were not enough, my daughter Gloria aroused in me a vague but constant anxiety because, although I had no fault to find with her, I felt all the time that there was, as they say, 'something wrong with her'. She was beautiful, extremely beautiful in fact, with a conspicuous, impressive kind of beauty and with a character that was naturally good, affectionate and submissive; and yet I was conscious of some mysterious flaw in her that made her weak-willed and inconstant in anything that she undertook. How many jobs she had started and then abandoned I couldn't begin to say. At twenty-seven she had already been a 'hostess', an interpreter, a secretary, an assistant in a boutique, a student in four different faculties, a hospital nurse, a baby-sitter. But what most disconcerted me in this life of perpetual failure was that Gloria did not seem to be in the least upset or frightened at it as, without doubt, I myself should have been in her place. On the contrary, she displayed a perfect and, to me, mysterious serenity as if she knew for certain that, beneath the mask of so many disappointments there lay hidden, reassuringly, a happy and fully successful vocation.

One day I had only just woken up from a restless, heavy sleep—the characteristic sleep of an unhappy woman like me—when the telephone rang. You must know that Gloria and I had a single telephone with communicating extensions, so that if I was telephoning Gloria could hear what I was saying and *vice versa*. So, with a sigh, I put out my hand in the darkness and took up the receiver, resigned, in anticipation, to being told that someone wished to speak to my daughter. But all this was no more than an expectation, for immediately, even before I opened my mouth, I was assaulted by a youthful, vehement voice that struck me—how shall I say?—by its nudity. It had some quality, that is, which suggested a person arriving in a drawing-room dressed in nothing but a pair of drawers. This 'nude' voice, by which I mean indecently sincere, passionate, physiological, did not give me time to clear up the misunderstanding; but without any preamble or transition discharged straight into my ear what I at once judged to be the drama of a humiliated lover. In short, what was it all about? A so-called 'confidence-trick', as far as I could understand, that is, an appointment which

Gloria had made and which she had then failed to keep. But this confidence-trick was not the first, there had been many others; and it was precisely about the excessive number of these confidence-tricks that the young man was complaining: one or two, no matter; but as many as this—no. Meanwhile, mingled with his reproofs, a certain amount of information was produced from which I was able to deduce that between him and Gloria there had been, and still was, a complete physical relationship.

My first impulse was to put the receiver back in place. But the frenzied, impassioned 'nudity' of the voice fascinated me; and so I went on listening as long as it was decently possible for me to do so. Then, at a somewhat peremptory demand ('You bitch, will you answer yes or no?') I assumed my most aristocratic and disdainful voice and said, 'Are you aware that you're speaking to Gloria's mother? I'll now transfer you to Gloria.' I called loudly to my daughter; but I did not put down the receiver. I gripped it convulsively in my hand on top of the coverlet. Then I made up my mind and held it up to my ear again.

I finished listening to the drama of the 'confidence-tricks' young man. Then, after a short interval, I intercepted the entirely different outpourings of another lover, this one, it seemed, more fortunate and more satisfied. The voice of the first speaker had been 'nude' in a disappointed and offensive manner; that of the second had the same quality but in a way that was grateful and passionate. He too provided very precise information on the completely intimate character of his relations with Gloria. More indiscreet because more favoured, he made frank allusions which several times almost led me to put down the receiver; but I resisted the temptation. After the two lovers, one unhappy and one happy, there was a brief conversation with a rather older man who made up for this by being very sure of himself. Finally a homely voice, the voice of a working-class young man, who asked Gloria, 'D'you remember me? I'm the one with the red sweater.' Gloria remembered him; and she listened to him, without showing any sign of impatience.

Gloria, as I knew, made and received telephone calls in the

early morning and, later, immediately after lunch. I no longer hesitated: as soon as we had cleared the table, I retired to my own room under the pretext of taking a siesta, impetuously took up the receiver and stuck it greedily to my ear. That afternoon the four callers of the morning telephoned again as well as three others, all of them involved with Gloria in some sort of obscure amorous intrigue. Then Gloria went out in order to go, as she told me, without doubt lying, to her English lesson; and I was left alone in the house to savour over again the bitter, troubled taste of my involuntary experience as a telephone spy. I felt ashamed of myself; and I swore to myself that I would not do it again. But next morning, at the first ring of the telephone bell, I seized hold of the receiver with a movement that was almost frantic. Finally, after a week, this had become a habit with me which I could no longer resist. But I justified it by telling myself that it was not so much curiosity that made me listen as the need to become absorbed in a reality different from my own, in fact in reality for its own sake.

And how did Gloria behave towards all those enamoured men's voices which followed and overlapped one another, each one ignorant of the others? She behaved in a curious manner, at the same time both prudent and provocative. She answered in monosyllables uttered, however, in a great variety of tones, or she would cut short her remarks halfway through as though she were afraid, or again she would say nothing, falling into a complete but nevertheless eloquent silence. For indeed, when she was not speaking it might be said that her body was speaking for her, her body which, in fact, while whichever man happened to be at the other end of the line was raving and becoming desperate, seemed to be breathing and throbbing into the receiver, as the sea is said to breathe and throb inside the shell that one holds in fun to one's ear.

One day at table I looked at Gloria and had the upsetting impression that I was seeing her for the first time. Above all I was struck by the extraordinary sweetness that seemed to emanate from her face and body. It was a sweetness that was entirely physiological and unconscious, of the same kind, I could not help thinking, as is characteristic of animals in the breeding season, and of flowers in spring.

First of all I had a feeling of repugnance, because I linked this sweetness with the ravings of all those men on the telephone. Though apparently passive and modest, the sweetness in reality had a quality of powerful, irresistible appeal. But then, almost at once, with the recall of a memory that crossed my mind, my repugnance gave place to an angry, impotent feeling of envy.

The memory that crossed my mind was, in fact, that I too, before my marriage, had had that same sweetness that Gloria had. But I, for some reason or other, had been ashamed of this sweetness and had decided to be rid of it as quickly as possible. So I married a young man of so-called 'good family' whom I did not love and who did not love me and then followed him in his career as a diplomat in embassies in many of the world's capital cities. And so, what happened to my sweetness? That's quickly told: it vanished in the fulfilment of social duties. It may be objected that social life is not a duty. It depends. It is one matter to welcome a few friends, freely and cheerfully, to one's own table; and quite another matter to entertain to dinner, for instance, about twenty members of a national delegation of some congress or other. Repeat a day of that sort for thirty years on end and then tell me whether it is an exaggeration to talk of duty.

While these thoughts were in my mind, I was still looking at Gloria and then I noticed another detail which annoyed and surprised me. In spite of all these men who telephoned to her and disputed her favours, she really seemed to be one of those girls who, in my time, were described by mothers as 'clean', 'wholesome' and 'bright'. To these very positive adjectives I would now, for my part, add another one: wise. Yes, Gloria had an air of wisdom, of wisdom that was almost stolid by dint of its reasonableness, and this mystified me completely. So that was how things stood between the two of us; she was the wise one and I was the fool. Truly the world was upside down.

At that moment my face must have had a distorted expression, for Gloria suddenly asked me, 'Why, Mum, what's the matter? What are you thinking about?'

I replied—I don't know why—'I was thinking that we ought to have the telephone changed. At the moment we can each of us listen to the other's conversations.'

She shrugged her shoulders, in a good-natured, indifferent way. 'What does it matter? No, we won't do that. Anyhow, I have no secrets from you, just as you have none from me.'

Shortly afterwards, with the usual pretext that I was tired and wanted to rest, I shut myself up in my room and impatiently lifted the receiver. I then heard the following conversation, 'But do you in fact think that someone is listening to us at this moment?'

'Yes, probably.'

'But you know what it is? A kind of voyeurism by hearing. Spying, in fact.'

'What does it matter to you? It makes no difference to us and it does her good. Since she's been listening to us she's become less hard, I might almost say she's become fond of me. And she's given up asking me to go with her to her insufferable receptions.'

These words hit me full in the face, so to speak, without my batting an eyelid. I settled myself more comfortably in my bed, stretched out my free arm to find the lamp-switch and turned off the light. In the dark, one listens better.

DEVOID OF INSTINCT

I have never married because I understood very early on
that anyone who, like me, thinks continually about love had
better keep well away from matrimony. Instead of marrying,
as so many women do, so as not to have to think about love,
I have taken on a profession, as an air hostess, which allows
me to support myself independently and to think about love
as much as I like without having to be accountable to anybody. I fly every day on the Middle Eastern routes, and all
the time that, smiling and attentive, I am doing the usual
things such as serving meals, superintending the fastening
of seat-belts, helping mothers in difficulties and so on, I am
thinking about love. Either I think about the love I have
had, or about the love I shall have. But this does not mean
that I am a woman of promiscuous tastes. On the contrary
I am almost completely inhibited. The fact is that I think a
great deal about love because it very rarely happens to me to
love or to be loved. At the age of thirty, pretty as I am, I
have had only a couple of important affairs. To make up for
that, however, I have never stopped thinking about love.

Sometimes I think that my lack of amorous instinct de-
rives from the profession I have chosen. I may be mistaken,
but it seems to me that, before I became a hostess, I can
remember being more sure of myself. The job of hostess has
made me into a rootless person, a person who no longer
knows where her home is, who hardly ever speaks her own
language, who lives for the most part up above the clouds,
in the eternal fine weather of the great heights. Whereas, in
order to love and be loved, we need roots. The peasant
woman, tied to the farmhouse and the fields, loves and is
loved; as is the shopkeeper who spends her time between her
home and her shop. But in the sky—how can one put down
roots in the sky? The saints, indeed, who always do the
opposite to us sinners, manage to do so. But how many
saints are there?

One night at Beirut—still owing to my continuous, inane thinking about love—I accepted an invitation to dinner from a pilot of my company, a man called Marco who had been importuning me for a long time, so as to see if by any chance he had the qualities needed to become, as they say, 'the man in my life'. I will give a description of this man Marco, if for no other reason than that he was my masculine ideal; and because, in spite of this, things went as they did. Marco, then, was one of those very fine-looking men in whom, however, an even excessive strength was balanced by an opposing quality; he was athletic but of gentle manners; brutal but melancholy; well-built but timid. At the most difficult moments he even stammered—a thing that I like and that gives me a feeling of tenderness.

We went to a restaurant of Oriental type with waiters in costume and furnishings in the Arab style; we sat down in a little courtyard with a marble basin and a fountain. We ordered a dinner of 'specialities' and then we confronted one another. My own situation was clear: I was there to be told that he loved me and perhaps even that he wanted to marry me; but just because it was clear, it alarmed me. Being entirely devoid of amorous instinct, with a very beautiful figure which on such occasions, however, regularly pretended to be deaf and refused to respond in any way, I was forced, to my great discomfort, by the idea that Marco was about to declare himself, into putting to myself what we may call the basic question: do I, in fact, like him or do I not? I looked at him, aware, as I did so, that I was making grimaces of perplexity which transformed my pretty 'hostess' face into a carnival mask; and the more I looked at him the less sure I felt. Now I was saying to myself, 'Yes, he's the man, he's really the man, there's no doubt that he is'; and then, on the other hand, 'No, no, he's not the man, for goodness' sake, he's not the right man, don't let us even talk about it.' Marco must have noticed something, for he asked me in a low voice, 'What's the matter? Some problem?'

'No, no problem. But don't let us be so silent. Let's talk.'

'I did actually have something to say to you.'

At once I was in a panic. 'Just *one* thing? But let's talk

about a lot of things. Talk to me about your native town.
Tell me where you were born. Tell me all about your family.'

Unwillingly he agreed; and I was disappointed because I
had for some reason imagined that he had his roots in some
little village, instead of which he was born in Milan, and he
talked about it, into the bargain, in a colourless, summary
fashion, like the typical man of few words that he was.
Meanwhile, however, he was trying to make me understand
that he loved me and could find no better way of doing so
than by staring at me with looks that were full of his own
stubborn, obtuse melancholy; while I, under this insistent
gaze, felt more and more nervous. Then the waiter brought
us a soup with mussels in it; I tried to open one of them
which was still closed; I was unsuccessful and broke one of
my fingernails; and then my irritation exploded. 'You see
this shellfish?' I said. 'Well, this evening you've turned me
into a shellfish like this one: just as tight-shut, just as obstinate, just as impervious.'

'But really, I . . .'

'Really you have invited me this evening to tell me that
you love me. Don't say no: I know it. And to make me
understand this you bombard me with looks like those of a
whipped dog. Well, it won't do, truly it won't do.'

'But what is it that won't do?'

'Your way of making a woman understand that you like
her.'

'Tell me yourself how I ought to behave.'

I gave a short, disagreeable laugh. And then, for some
reason, I made up my mind to teach him what I myself
knew nothing about. 'No glances, no smiles, no hand-caress-
ings, no *courtship*, in fact. Who goes in for *courtship* nowa-
days? What you should aim at is mathematical love-
making.'

He seemed astonished, and repeated: '*Mathematical* love-
making? What is mathematical love-making?'

Having now initiated the subject, I replied, 'It's the kind
of love-making that does not go through the phase of
glances and compliments and smiles and so forth. It's like
a mathematical exercise: I like this woman; she likes me; so

these two likings must be added together to make the total, which means doing exactly the thing that needs to be done.'

'What thing?'

'The thing.'

He fell into a heavy, meditative silence; no doubt he found this matter of mathematical love-making difficult to swallow. We finished eating almost without speaking; then I told him curtly that I was tired and he paid the bill; and we walked away, still in silence, to the hotel which was not far off. I took my key from the porter, and my perplexity now was so deep that even the porter noticed the harsh grimace of indecision which disfigured my face. I felt I must put Marco to the test, the final test, and invited him to accompany me up to my floor. In the lift I stood back and leant against the wall; but secretly I was crying out, 'Come on, seize hold of me, come on, what are you waiting for?' But nothing happened; and this was a good thing because I felt that if he had 'seized hold of me' as I desired, my absurd but inevitable reply would have been a hard slap in the face.

The lift came to a stop; biting my lower lip with rage, I got out and went with lowered head to the door of my room. Marco joined me; I turned round with a jerk and found myself with my mouth almost against his mouth and then, at last, we kissed. The kiss was of less than mediocre quality, so much so that I had time to think, 'No, he's not the man, he is absolutely *not* the man.' Then we separated and I glanced over Marco's shoulder along the corridor to the point where there were two lifts. One of them, our lift, was going down; but the doors of the other were open and a man was watching me and I realized that he had seen us kissing. He was a fair-haired man of middle age, his hair cut short and with a forelock; he had a red face and blue eyes with a slight squint. He was small but robust; with bell-bottomed blue trousers and a short-sleeved shirt with anchors on it: a sailor, evidently. Then, possibly for the first time in my life, the instinct which I did not think I possessed made itself felt clearly and precisely. I whispered to Marco, 'There are people, you must go away; we'll see each other tomorrow';

and I shook him by the hand and almost pushed him away. Marco ran off, drunk with happiness, and I stooped down to put the key into the lock of my door. But my hand was trembling, still owing to that instinct which had at last been aroused; and I could not manage to insert the key and at the same time I felt that the sailor was coming up behind my back. I said to myself, 'Let's hope he really did see us and that he'll feel encouraged to find himself lacking in respect for me'; and then a thick red hand with fair hairs on the back of it slipped over my hand, took the key and inserted it firmly into the keyhole. The door opened, the man pushed me into my room, shut the door behind me and turned on the light.

Mathematical! Everything had happened just exactly as in a mathematical exercise. But when I saw the man with the fair forelock making his way towards me with his hands outstretched to seize hold of me, with his blue trousers and his shirt with the anchors on it and a smile that displayed his teeth, my instinct faded away completely and I cried, 'Don't come near me!'

Sure of himself, he shook his head and took another step forward. Then I retreated to the bathroom door, reached down in a great hurry into the bath, snatched up the pipe of the shower, turned on the tap and aimed the jet of water at him. It was a very modern hotel; and it was a powerful jet. Like a true sailor accustomed to the waves of the sea, he remained unperturbed, his face scarlet and erect in the jet of water that flooded him. Then he took a step back, as if to reassure me, without haste and without anger. He said, in English, 'I'm sorry, I thought...'

I answered, also in English, 'You thought that, since that other man had given me a kiss, you could go to bed with me. Isn't that so?'

'Yes, perhaps.'

'Well, go away, go away at once. Otherwise I shall start screaming.'

I don't know why he then asked me of what nationality I was. Still keeping an eye on him with the pipe of the shower in my hand, I told him. He said, for form's sake, that he liked Rome very much; then he made me a slight bow and went away.

Now I was alone. Marco had been timid and sentimental and I had not liked him; the sailor had been 'mathematical' and I had not liked him either. I went over the looking-glass, gazed at myself and said aloud, 'Devoid of instinct!'